Shakespeare

King Henry IV
Part I

SALZWASSER
VERLAG

Shakespeare

King Henry IV
Part I

1st Edition | ISBN: 978-3-75250-182-7

Place of Publication: Frankfurt am Main, Germany

Year of Publication: 2020

Salzwasser Verlag GmbH, Germany.

Reprint of the original, first published in 1869.

SHAKESPEARE'S

HISTORICAL PLAY

The First Part of

KING HENRY IV,

AS PRODUCED AT

BOOTH'S THEATRE,

Monday, November 29, 1869.

—————•◆•—————

NEW YORK:

SAMUEL FRENCH, PUBLISHER,

122 NASSAU STREET.

FRENCH'S STANDARD DRAMA.

No. LXXV

—

KING HENRY IV.

PART I.

A TRAGEDY.

IN FIVE ACTS.

BY WILLIAM SHAKSPEARE.

ALSO,

THE STAGE BUSINESS, CASTS OF CHARACTERS, COSTUMES, RELATIVE POSITIONS, ETC.

NEW YORK:

SAMUEL FRENCH, PUBLISHER.

122 NASSAU STREET, (UP STAIRS.)

CAST OF CHARACTERS.

	Covent Garden.	Walnut St 1843.	Arch St 1848.	Park 1843
King Henry IV.	Mr. Everton.	Mr. Heakins.	Mr. Henkins	Mr. Barry.
Prince of Wales.	" C Kemble.	" Wheatley.	" Thayer.	" Hield.
Prince John....	" J Matthews.	" Miss Price.	Miss Morgen,	Miss Flynn.
Sir John Falstaff	" Yates	" W. R. Blake.	Mr. W. R Blake	Mr. Hacket & Ba
Westmoreland ..	" Conner.	" G. Branne.	" Calladine.	" Rec.
Douglas........	" Claremont.	" Davenport.	" Wood.	" Stark.
Worcester......	" Chapman.	" McKeon.	" Elesler.	" Dougherty.
Northumberland.	" B Thornton.	" Duff.	" Jarvis.	" Anderson.
Hotspur........	" Macready.	" J Wallack, Jr	" March.	" Dyott.
Sir W. Blunt ...	" Conner.	" Young.	" Meara.	" Pearson.
Sir R. Vernon..	" Abbott.	" Brunton.	" Worrell.	" A. Anderson
Sheriff..........	" Jeffries.	" Neil.	" Bradford.	
Poins...........	" Farley.	" Laman.	" T. B Johston	" McDonald.
Bardolph.......	" Atkins.	" Radcliff.	" W. E Burton	" Povey.
Gadshill........		" Eberle.	" Thompson.	" Heath.
Peto		" Stevens.	" Dickson.	" Nelson.
Francis........	" Simmons.	" Chapman.	Master Wood.	" W Chapman
First Carrier...	" Faucit.	" Spear.		" G Andrews
Second Carrier..	" Treby.	" C. Foster.		" Gallot.
Lady Perry.....	Miss Foote	" Mrs. J Wallack	Miss Wood.	Mrs. Abbott.
Dame Quickly ..	Mrs. Davenport	Mrs. Jones.	Mrs. Hughes.	" Vernon.

COSTUMES.

KING HENRY.—Brown velvet robe, scarlet and gold trunks, puffed with white satin, white silk pantaloons, white shoes, with scarlet roses, splendid hat, and white plumes.

PRINCE OF WALES.—Brown tunic buff pantaloons, russet boots, drab colored hat, and black plumes. Second dress.—White court dress, richly embroidered with silver. Third dress—a complete suit of armour.

PRINCE JOHN.—Light blue jacket, white pantaloons, russet boots; round hat and white plumes.

WORCESTER —Crimson velvet dress, crimson and gold trunks, puffed with white satin, white pantaloons, russet boots, black hat, and white plumes.

NORTHUMBERLAND.—Green velvet dress, with trunks, &c., (see Worcestor.)

DOUGLAS.—Tartan plaid, kelt bonnet, and breast plate.

HOTSPUR.—Purple velvet jacket, richly embroidered, black satin mantle,— scarlet pantaloons, russet boots. Second dress—complete armour.

WESTMORELAND.—Crimson old English dress, black hat, and white plumes.

SIR RICHARD VERNON.—Light blue old English dress.

SIR WALTER BLUNT.—Scarlet ditto

SIR JOHN FALSTAFF.—Buff, scarlet and white ditto.

POINS.—Common blue ditto.

RABY.—Light blue ditto.

FRANCIS.—Brown ditto.

BARDOLPH.—Dark brown, slightly trimmed with scarlet.

GADSHILL.—Brown PETO,—Blue common dress.

SHERIFF—Scarlet gown and gold chain.

LADY PERCY.—Plain white satin.

DAME QUICKLY.—Scarlet stuff petticoat, flowered gown, white apron, high and sharp crowned hat, trimmed with scarlet.

EDITORIAL INTRODUCTION.

This celebrated and most attractive of all the plays of Shakspeare is so often enacted, and it is so well known to the whole world, that it is scarcely necessary to say one word in reference to it, by the way of editorial introduction. At what time the great master of nature produced it, is not now known ; but it is gener_ally supposed that it was originally played in the life-time of Shakespeare ; and, there is a tradition extant, among the writings of the old players, that he himself enacted the part of Hotspur at Globe Theatre, London, in the year 1597. But, as it is recorded by almost all the dramatic biographical writers, from old John Dennis down to Mr. Victor, that the ghost in Hamlet, was the climax of his ambition as an actor, the report referred to, does not seem to be founded on probability. It is generally supposed that the first and second parts of King Henry IV. were originally written at the same time : the one being but a continuation of the other; but, that being found too bulky for a single representation, they were subsequently divided.

It is difficult to say which of the two parts is most attractive, since it is universally admitted that both contain some of the most beautiful passages of passion and poetry that can be found in all the works of the mighty Bard of Avon. What, for instance can be more eloquent or beautiful than Hotspur's reply to Sir Walter Blunt, in the First Part, when that nobleman appeals to him in the name of royalty, to lay down the weapons of rebellion and accept the Regal Pardon !

> HOT. The king is kind : and well we know, the king
> Knows at what time to promise, when to pay.
> My father, and my uncle, and myself
> Did give him that same royalty he wears :
> And---when he was not six and twenty strong,
> Sick in the world's regard, wretched and low,
> A poor unminded out-law sneaking home---
> My father gave him welcome to the shore :
> And---when he heard him swear and vow to heaven,
> He came but to be Duke of Lancaster---
> My father, in kind heart and pity moved,
> Swore him assistance, and performed it too,
> Now, when the lords and barons of the realm
> Perceived Northumberland did lean to him,
> The more and less came in with cap and knee.
> Met him in boroughs, cities, villages ;

Laid gifts before him, proffered him their oaths,
Gave him their heirs; as pages followed him.
Even at the heels, in golden multitudes.
He presently, as greatness knows itself,
Stnps me a little higher than his vaw
Made to my father while his blood was poor,
Upon the naked shore at Ravenspurg;
And now, forsooth, takes on him to reform
Some certain edicts, nud some strait decrees,
That be too heavy opon the commonwealth ;
Cries out upon abuses. seems to weep
Over his country's wrongs ; and by his face,
This seeming brow of justice, did he win
The hearts of all that he did angle fur.

It were idle, however, to pause to select the beauties combined in this remarkble production : it is literally a succession of poetical diamonds. There is not a character in it, from King Henry VI to Bardolph, that does not sparkle with the scintillations of wit and poetry; and, whilst we are at one moment lost in the admiration the bold eloquence and noble daring Hotspur elicits, we are at the next convulsed with laughter, which the keen wit and satire of the fat knight, Sir John Falstaff, engenders.

It is not probable that Shakspeare intended that Sir John Falstaff should carry off the glory of the piece, or be regarded as the "bright particular star," who should keep a whole audience in restless anxiety for his appearance before them. It is said by the old chroniclers that he had a personal object, blended with revenge in view, when he introduced Falstaff to the play, who was a real personage, and had incurred the displeasure of the Immortal Bard.

But it is idle, to suppose that Shakspeare had any invidious designs in view, when he conceived and executed the character of Falstaff. It is admitted on all hands that his original Sir John Falstaff, died in the year 1469, ninety-five years before the great Bard was born, and one hundred and fifty-seven in anticipation of his death. It is not unlikely that he might have taken the history of Falstaff for his model, inasmuch as that celebrated man had had his order of knighthood taken from him, by the Duke of Hereford, in consequence of the cowardice he displayed in flying from Joan of Arc, the Maid of Orleans. Sir John Falstaff is now a familiar character with the public and the profession, and is often attempted by actors, who do not possess a solitary talent for the part. Quinn, was many years the only recognised Falstaff on the English Stage, and few dared at tempt the character till after that celebrated man died in the year 1676. After his death, there were numerous Falstaffs ; but Stephen Kemble, who played the part for the last time in the year 1813, was probably the most successful in securing the fame of the world. In this country, the late Mr. Warren, of Philadelphia was for many years the recognised Falstaff; though, the late' John Dwyer, William Jones, and Thomas Cooper, besides many others, were considered respectable, as the representatives of the fat knight of the Boar's Head in East Cheap. Mr. James H. Hackett, is now by many regarded, as the most perfect Falstaff extant. The critics, however, differ very materially in their opinions, and we are not disposed to discuss the subject

KING HENRY IV.

PART I.

ACT I.

SCENE I.—*The Palace in London.—Flourish of Trumpets and Drums.*

KING HENRY, C., *seated on his Throne*, PRINCE JOHN-OF LANCASTER, EARL OF WESTMORELAND, SIR RICHARD VERNON, SIR WALTER BLUNT, *and Attendants, discovered.*

King H. So shaken as we are, so wan with care,
Find we a time for frighted peace to pant.
Therefore, friends,
Forthwith a power of English shall we levy,
To chase these pagans from the holy fields.
Then let me hear
Of you, my gentle cousin Westmoreland,
What yesternight our council did decree,
In forwarding this dear expedience.
West. (R.) My liege, this haste was hot in question,
And many limits of the charge set down
But yesternight : when, all athwart, there came
A post from Wales, loaden with heavy news ;
Whose worst was, that the noble Mortimer,
Leading the men of Herefordshire to fight
Against the irregular and wild Glendower,
Was by the rude hands of that Welchman taken,
And a thousand of his people butchered.
King H. It seems, then, that the tidings of this broil
Brake off our business for the Holy Land.
West. This matched with other, did, my gracious lord

For more uneven and unwelcome news
Came from the North, and thus it did import:
On Holyrood day, the gallant Hotspur there,
Young Harry Percy, and brave Archibald,
That ever-valiant and approvéd Scot,
At Holmedon met,
Where they did spend a sad and bloody hour:
As by discharge of their artillery,
And shape of likelihood, the news was told;
For he that brought them, in the very heat
And pride of their contention did take horse,
Uncertain of the issue any way.

    King H. [*Pointing,* L., *to Sir Walter Blunt.*] Here is a
        dear, a true-industrious friend,
Sir Walter Blunt, new-lighted from his horse,
And he hath brought us smooth and welcome news.
The Earl of Douglas is discomfited
On Holmedon's plains: of prisoners, Hotspur took
Mordake the Earl of Fife, and eldest son
To beaten Douglas; and the Earls
Of Athol, Murray, Angus, and Monteith.
And is not this an honourable spoil?
A gallant prize? ha, cousin, is it not?

    West. It is a conquest for a prince to boast of.
    King H. Yea, there thou mak'st me sad, and mak'st me
        sin,
In envy that my Lord Northumberland
Should be the father of so blessed a son,
Whilst I, by looking on the praise of him,
See riot and dishonour stain the brow
Of my young Harry. Oh, that it could be proved
That some night-tripping fairy had exchanged
In cradle-clothes our children where they lay,
And called mine—Percy, his—Plantaganet!
Then would I have his Harry, and he mine.
But let him from my thoughts:—what think you, coz',
Of this young Percy's pride? the prisoners,
Which he in this adventure hath surprised,
To his own use he keeps: and sends me word,
I shall have none but Mordake, Earl of Fife.

    West. This is his uncle's teaching, this is Worcester,
Malevolent to you in all aspects.

King H. But I have sent for him to answer this ;
And, for this cause, [*Rising.*] awhile we must neglect
Our holy purpose to Jerusalem.
Cousin, on Wednesday next, our council we
Will hold at Windsor, so inform the lords :
But come yourself [*Going*, L.] with speed to us again ;
For more is to be said, and to be done,
Than out of anger can be uttered.

> [*Flourish of Trumpets.—Exeunt, Westmoreland*, R.,
> *the others*, L.

Scene II.—*An Apartment belonging to the Prince of Wales.*

Enter Prince of Wales, L., *and* Sir John Falstaff R.

Fal. [*Both* R. C.) Now, Hal, what time of day is it,
lad ?

Prince H. Thou art so fat-witted, with drinking of old
sack, and unbuttoning thee after supper, and sleeping upon benches after noon, that thou hast forgotten to demand
that truly which thou wouldst truly know. What a devil
hast thou to do with the time of the day ? Unless hours
were cups of sack, and minutes capons, and clocks the
tongues of bawds ; I see no reason why thou should'st be
so superfluous, to demand the time of the day.

Fal. Indeed, you come near me now, Hal; for we, that
take purses, go by the moon and seven stars ; and not by
Phœbus—he, that wand'ring knight so fair. And, I pray
thee, sweet wag, when thou art king, as heaven save thy
grace, (majesty, I should say ; for grace thou wilt have
none)—

Prince H. [*Starting back to* c.] What ! none !

Fal. (R. C.) No, by my troth ; not so much as will serve
to be prologue to an egg and butter.

Prince H. [*Returning to Falstaff*, R. C.] Well, how,
then ? come, roundly, roundly.

Fal. Marry, then, sweet wag, when thou art king, let
not us, that are squires of the night's body, be called
thieves of the day's beauty ; let us be—Diana foresters,
gentlemen of the shade, minions of the moon : and let
men say, we be men of good government ; being governed,
as the sea is, by our noble and chaste mistress, the moon,
under whose countenance we—steal.

[Pushing the Prince with his stick to c.

Prince H. (c.) Thou say'st well; and it holds well, too; for the fortune of us, that are the moon's men, doth ebb and flow like the sea; being governed, as the sea is, by the moon. As, for proof, now: a purse of gold most resolutely snatched on Monday night, and most dissolutely spent on Tuesday morning; got with swearing—lay by; and spent with crying—bring in: now, in as low an ebb as the foot of the ladder, and, by and by, in as high a flow as the ridge of the gallows.

Fal. By the lord, thou say'st true, lad. And is not my hostess of the tavern a most sweet wench?

Prince H. As the honey of Hybla, my old lad of the castle. And is not a buff jerkin a most sweet robe of durance? *[Tapping Falstaff's belly with his cane.*

Fal. How now, how now, mad wag? what, in thy quips, and thy quiddities? what a plague have I to do with a buff jerkin?

Prince H. Why, what a plague have I to do with my hostess of the tavern?

Fal. Well, thou hast called her to a reckoning many a time and oft.

Prince H. [*Leaning on Falstaff's shoulder*] Did I ever call for thee to pay thy part?

Fal. No; I'll give thee thy due, thou hast paid all there?

Prince H. Yea, and elsewhere, so far as my coin would stretch: and, where it would not, I have used my credit.

Fal. (n.) Yea, and so used it, that, were it not here apparent that thou art heir apparent. But, I pr'ythee, sweet wag, shall there be gallows standing in England when thou art king? and resolution thus fobbed as it is, with the rusty curb of old father antick the law? Do not thou, when thou art king, hang a thief.

Prince H. No; thou shalt.

Fal. Shall I? Oh, rare! By the lord, I'll be a brave judge.

Prince H. Thou judgest false already; I mean, thou shalt have the hanging of the thieves, and so become a rare hangman.

Fal. Well, Hal, well; and in some sort it jumps with my humour, as well as waiting in the court, I can tell you.

Prince H. For obtaining of suits?

Fal. Yea, for obtaining of suits; whereof the hangman hath no 'ean wardrobe. [*Shaking his head and crossing,* c.] 'Sblood, I am as melancholy as a gib-cat, or a lugged bear.

Prince H. Or an old lion; or a lover's lute.

Fal. (c.) Yea, or the drone of a Lincolnshire bagpipe.

Prince H. (n. c.) What say'st thou to a hare, or the melancholy of Moor-ditch?

Fal. Thou hast the most unsavoury similies; and art, indeed, the most comparative, rascalliest—sweet young prince—but, Hal, I pr'ythee, trouble me no more with vanity. I would to heaven thou and I knew where a commodity of good names were to be bought: an old lord of the council rated me the other day in the street about you, sir; but I marked him not; and yet he talked very wisely; but I regarded him not; and yet he talked wisely, and in the street, too.

Prince H. Thou didst well; for wisdom cries out in the streets, and no man regards it.

Fal. Oh, thou hast damnable iteration; and art, indeed, able to corrupt a saint. Thou hast done much harm upon me, Hal—[*Turns to* n., *laughing.*]—Heaven forgive thee for it! Before I knew thee, Hal, I knew nothing; and now am I, if a man should speak truly, little better than one of the wicked. [*Crosses,* R. c.] I must give over this life, and I will give it over; by the lord, an I do not I am a villain; I'll be damned for never a king's son in Christendom.

Prince H. (c.) Where shall we take a purse to-morrow, Jack?

Fal. [*After a short pause eagerly shakes hands with the Prince.*] Where thou wilt, lad, I'll make one; an I do not, call me villain, and baffle me.

Prince H. I see a good amendment of life in thee; from praying to purse-taking.

Fal. Why, Hal, 'tis my vocation, Hal; 'tis no sin for a man to labour in his vocation.

Enter POINS, L.

Prince H. Good morrow, Ned.

Poins. Good morrow, sweet Hal. What says Monsieur

Remorse ? [*Crosses to Falstaff*, R.] What says Sir John Sack-and-Sugar ? [*Going*, L.] But, my lads, my lads, tomorrow morning, by four o'clock, early at Gadshill—There are pilgrims going to Canterbury with rich offerings, and traders riding to London with fat purses; I have visors for you all, you have horses for yourselves: (L.) Gadshill lies to night in Rochester: I have bespoke supper in Eastcheap: we may do it as secure as sleep : if you will go, I will stuff your purses full of crowns; if you will not, tarry at home, and be hanged.

Fal. (R.) Hear me, Yedward ; if I tarry at home, and go not, I'll hang you for going.

Poins. You will, chops ?

Fal. [*Crossing*, C.] Hal, wilt thou make one ?

Prince H. Who, I rob? I a thief? not I, by my faith.

Poins. There's neither honesty, manhood, nor good fellowship in thee ; nor thou camest not of the blood royal, if thou darest not stand for ten shillings.

Prince H. Well, then, once in my days I'll be a mad cap.

Fal. Why, that's well said.

Prince H. [*Going*, R.]Well, come what will, I'll tarry at home.

Fal. (L. C.) By the lord, I'll be a traitor, then, when thou art king.

Prince H. (R. S. E.) I care not.

[*Leaning thoughtfully against a pillar.*

Poins. (L. C.) Sir John, I pr'ythee, leave the Prince and me alone ; I will lay him down such reasons for this adventure, that he shall go.

Fal. Well, may'st thou have the spirit of persuasion, and he the ears of profiting ; that what thou speakest may move, and what he hears may be believed ; (L.) that the true Prince may, for recreation sake, prove a false thief; for the poor abuses of the time want countenance. [*Prince returns*, C.] Farewell: you shall find me in Eastcheap.

Prince H. (L.) Farewell, thou latter spring ! farewell, All-hallown summer !   [*Exit Falstaff*, L.

Poins. Now, my good sweet honey lord, ride with us to-morrow ; I have a jest to execute, that I cannot manage alone. Falstaff, Bardolph, Peto, and Gadshill shall rob those men that we have already waylaid; yourself and I will not be there : and, when they have the booty, if you and I do not rob them, cut this head from my shoulders.

Prince H. (L. C.) But how shall we part with them in setting forth ?

Poins. (C.) Why, we will set forth before, or after them, and appoint them a place of meeting, wherein it is at our pleasure to fail ; and then will they adventure upon the exploit themselves : which they shall have no sooner achieved, but we'll set upon them.

Prince H. Ay, but 'tis like that they will know us by our horses, by our habits, and by every other appointment, to be ourselves.

Poins. Tut ! our horses they shall not see ; I'll tie them in the wood ; our visors we will change, after we leave them ; and I have cases of buckram, for the nonce, to unmask our noted outward garments.

Prince H. But 1 doubt they will be too hard for us.

Poins. Well, for two of them, I know them to be as noted cowards as ever turned back ; and for the third, if he fight longer than he sees reason, I'll forswear arms. The virtue of this jest will be, the incomprehensible lies that this same fat rogue will tell us when we meet at supper : how thirty, at least, he fought with ; what wards, what blows, what extremities he endured ; and in the reproof of this lies the jest.

Prince H. Well, I'll go with thee : provide us all things necessary, and meet me in Eastcheap : farewell.

Poins. Farewell, my lord. [*Exit,* L.

Prince H. (R. C.) I know you all, and will awhile up-
  hold
The unyoked humour of your idleness :
Yet herein will I imitate the sun ;
Who doth permit the base contagious clouds
To smother up his beauty from the world ;
That when he please again to be himself,
Being wanted, he may be more wondered at,
By breaking through the foul and ugly mists
Of vapours that did seem to strangle him. (C.)
So, when this loose behaviour 1 throw off,
And pay the debt 1 never promised,
By how much better than my word I am,

By so much shall I falsify men's hopes :
And, like bright metal on a sullen ground,
My reformation, glittering o'er my fault,
Shall show more goodly, and attract more eyes
Than that which hath no foil to set it off. (L. c.)
I'll so offend, to make offence a skill ;
Redeeming time when men least think I will. [*Exit*, L.

SCENE III.—*The Council Chamber.—Flourish of Trumpets and Drums.*

KING HENRY, PRINCE JOHN, EARL OF WESTMORELAND, EARL OF WORCESTER, EARL OF NORTHUMBERLAND, HOTSPUR, SIR WALTER BLUNT, SIR RICHARD VERNON, *and other Gentlemen, Guards, and Attendants.*

King H. [*Seated on the Throne,* c.] My blood hath been
    too cold and temperate,
Unapt to stir at these indignities,
And you have found me ; for, accordingly,
You tread upon my patience ; but, be sure,
I will from henceforth rather be myself,
Mighty, and to be feared, than my condition,
Which hath been smooth as oil, soft as young down :
And therefore lost that title of respect,
Which the proud soul ne'er pays but to the proud.

Wor. (L.) Our house, my sovereign liege, little deserves
The scourge of greatness to be used on it ;
And that same greatness, too, which our own hands
Have holp to make so portly.

Nor. (R. S. F.) My lord—

King H. [*Hastily rising.*]. Worcester, get thee gone;
    for I do see
Danger and disobedience in thine eye :
Oh, sir,
Your presence is too bold and peremptory ;
And majesty might never yet endure
The bloody frontier of a servant brow.
You have good leave to leave us : when we need
Your use and counsel, we shall send for you.

                [*Sits.—Exit Worcester,* L.

[*To Northumberland.*] You were about to speak.

Nor. Yea, my good lord.

Those prisoners in your highness' name demanded
Which Harry Percy here at Holmedon took,
Were, as he says, not with such strength denied,
As is delivered to your Majesty.

Hot. (R.) My liege, I did deny no prisoners.
But, I remember, when the fight was done,
When I was dry with rage, and extreme toil,
Breathless and faint, leaning upon my sword,
Came there a certain lord, neat, trimly dressed,
Fresh as a bridegroom; and his chin new reaped,
Showed like a stubble-land at harvest home:
He was perfumed like a milliner:
And 'twixt his finger and thumb he held
A pouncet-box, which ever and anon
He gave his nose, and took't away again;
And still he smiled, and talked:
And, as the soldiers bore dead bodies by,
He called them—untaught knaves, unmannerly,
To bring a slovenly, unhandsome corse
Betwixt the wind and his nobility.
With many holiday and lady terms
He questioned me; among the rest, demanded
My prisoners, in your Majesty's behalf.
I then, all smarting, with my wounds being cold,
Out of my grief, and my impatience,
To be so pestered with a poppinjay,
Answered neglectingly, I know not what:
He should, or he should not; for he made me mad,
To see him shine so brisk, and smell so sweet,
And talk, so like a waiting gentlewoman,
Of guns, and drums, and wounds,—(Heaven save the
        mark!)—
And telling me, the sovereign'st thing on earth
Was parmaceti for an inward bruise;
And that it was great pity, so it was,
That villainous saltpetre should be digged
Out of the bowels of the harmless earth,
Which many a good tall fellow had destroyed
So cowardly; and but for these vile guns,
He would himself have been a soldier.
This bald unjointed chat of his, my lord,
I answered indirectly, as I said:

And, I beseech you, let not his report
Come current for an accusation,
Betwixt my love and your high majesty.

Blunt. (L.) The circumstance considered, good my lord,
Whatever Harry Percy then had said,
To such person, and in such a place,
At such a time, with all the rest re-told,
May reasonably die, and never rise
To do him wrong, or any way impeach
What he then said, so he unsay it now.

King H. Why, yet he doth deny his prisoners;
But with proviso, and exception,
That we, at our own charge, shall ransom straight
His brother-in-law, the foolish Mortimer;
Who, on my soul, hath wilfully betrayed
The lives of those that he did lead to fight
Against the great magician, damned Glendower:
Whose daughter, as we hear, the Earl of March
Hath lately married. Shall our coffers, then,
Be emptied to redeem a traitor home?
Shall we buy treason? and indent with fears,
When they have lost and forfeited themselves?
No, on the barren mountains let him starve;
For I shall never hold that man my friend,
Whose tongue shall ask me for one penny cost
To ransom home revolted Mortimer.

Hot. (R.) Revolted Mortimer!
He never did fall off, my sovereign liege,
But by the chance of war: [*Nearer the King.*] To prove
     that true,
Needs no more but one tongue for all those wounds,
Those mouthéd wounds, which valiantly he took,
When on the gentle Severn's sedgy bank,
In single opposition, hand to hand,
He did confound the best part of an hour
In changing hardiment with great Glendower:
Three times they breathed, [*Returns,* R.] and three times
     did they drink,
Upon agreement, of swift Severn's flood;
Who then, affrighted with their bloody looks,
Ran fearfully among the trembling reeds,
And his crisp head in the hollow bank,

Blood-stained with these valiant combatants,
Never did base and rotten policy
Colour her working with such deadly wounds;
Nor never could the noble Mortimer
Receive so many, and all willingly;
Then let him not be slandered with revolt.

King H. Thou dost belie him, Percy, [*Rising.*] thou
    dost belie him,
He never did encounter with Glendower:
I tell thee,   [*Advancing,* c.
He durst as well have met the devil alone,
As Owen Glendower for an enemy.
Art not ashamed? But, sirrah, henceforth
Let me not hear you speak of Mortimer.
Send me your prisoners with the speediest means,
Or you shall hear in such a kind from me
As will displease you. My lord Northumberland,
We license your departure with your son :   [*Going,* L
Send us your prisoners, or you'll hear of it.

    [*Flourish of Trumpets and Drums.—Exeunt all but
    Northumberland and Hotspur,* L.

Hot. (L. c.) And if the devil come and roar for them,
I will not send them :—[*North. stands* R.] I will after
    straight,
And tell him so; for I will ease my heart,
Although it be with hazard of my head.   [*Going,* L.

Nor. [*Following.*] What, drunk with choler? stay and
    pause awhile;
Here comes your uncle.

        Enter WORCESTER, L.

Hot. Speak of Mortimer?
Yes, I will speak of him: and let my soul
Want mercy if I do not join with him:
Yea, on his part, I'll empty all these veins,
And shed my dear blood drop by drop i'the dust,
But I will lift the down-trod Mortimer
As high i' the air as this unthankful king,
As this ingrate and cankered Bolingbroke.

Nor. Brother, the king hath made your nephew mad.

Wor. Who struck this heat up after I was gone?

Hot. (R.) I cannot blame him: was he not proclaimed

By Richard that dead is, the next of blood?

    Nor. (R.) He was; I heard the proclamation;
And then it was, when the unhappy king
(Whose wrongs in us heaven pardon!) did set forth
Upon his Irish expedition;
From whence he, intercepted, did return,
To be deposed, and, shortly, murdered.

    Hot. (C.) But soft, I pray you: did King Richard then
Proclaim my brother Edmund Mortimer
Heir to the crown?

    Nor. He did; myself did hear it.

    Hot. Nay, then I cannot blame his cousin king,
That wished him on the barren mountains starved.
But shall't, for shame, be spoken in these days,
Or fill up chronicles in time to come,
That men of your nobility and power,
Did 'gage them both in an unjust behalf,
(As both of you, heaven pardon it! have done),
To put down Richard, that sweet lovely rose,
And plant this thorn, this canker, Bolingbroke?
And shall it, in more shame, be further spoken,
That you are fooled, discarded, and shook off
By him, for whom these shames ye underwent?
No; yet time serves, wherein you may redeem
Your banished honours, and restore yourselves
Into the good thoughts of the world again:
Revenge the jeering and disdained contempt
Of this unthankful king; who studies, day and night
To answer all the debt he owes to you,
Even with the bloody payment of your deaths:
Therefore, I say—

    Wor. Peace, cousin, say no more:
And now I will unclasp a secret book,
And in your quick conceiving discontents
I'll read you matter deep and dangerous;
As full of peril, and advent'rous spirit,
As to o'erwalk a current, roaring loud,
On the unsteadfast footing of a spear.

    Hot. If he fall in, good night:—or sink, or swim:
Send danger from the east unto the west,
So honour cross it from the north to south,
And let them grapple:—Oh! the blood more stirs,

To rouse a lion than to start a hare.   [*Crosses,* R.

Nor. (c.) Imagination of some great exploit
Drives him beyond the bounds of patience.

Hot. (R.) By heaven, methinks it were an easy 'eap
To pluck bright honour from the pale-faced moon ;
Or dive into the bottom of the deep,
Where fathom-line could never touch the ground,
And pluck up drownéd honour by the locks ;
So he, that doth redeem her thence, might wear,
Without corrival, all her dignities :—
But out upon this half-faced fellowship !

Wor. (R.) He apprehends a world of figures here,
But not the form he should attend.—
Good cousin, give me audience for a while.

Hot. I cry your mercy.

Wor. Those same noble Scots,
That are your prisoners—

Hot. (c.) I'll keep them all :
By heaven, he shall not have a Scot of them ;
No, if a Scot would save his soul he shall not :
I'll keep them, by this hand.

Wor. (L.) You start away,
And lend no ear unto my purposes :
Those prisoners you shall keep.

Hot. Nay, I will ; that's flat :—
He said, he would not ransom Mortimer ;
Forbad my tongue to speak of Mortimer ;
But I will find him when he lies asleep,
And in his ear I'll holla—Mortimer !—Nay,
I'll have a starling shall be taught to speak
Nothing but Mortimer, and give it him,
To keep his anger still in motion.   [*Crosses,* R

Wor. Farewell, kinsman ! I will talk to you
When you are better tempered to attend.

North. Why, what a wasp-stung and impatient fool
Art thou, to break into this woman's mood,
Tying thine ear to no tongue but thine own !

Hot. (R) Why look you, I am whipped and scourged
        with rods,
Nettled, and stung with pismires, when I hear
Of this vile politician, Bolingbroke. (c.)
In Richard's time—What do you call the place ?—

A plague upon't !—it is in Glostershire ;
'Twas where the mad-cap duke his uncle kept ;
His uncle York ;—where first I bow'd my knee
Unto this king of smiles, this Bolingbroke ;—
When you and he came back from Ravenspurg.

North. (R. C.) At Berkley Castle.

Hot. You say true :—
Why, what a candy deal of courtesy
This fawning greyhound then did proffer me !
Look—when his infant fortune came to age—
And—gentle Harry Percy—and, kind cousin—
O. the devil take such cozeners !　Heaven forgive me
Good uncle, tell your tale, for I have done.

Wor. (L. C.) Nay, if you have not, to't again ;
We'll stay your leisure.

Hot. I have done, i'faith.

Wor. Then once more to your Scottish prisoners.
Deliver them up without their ransoms straight,
And make the Douglas' son your only mean
For powers in Scotland ; which, (for divers reasons
Which I shall send you written,) be assured,
Will easily be granted.—You, my lord—(*To* NORTH.)
Your son in Scotland being thus employed—
Shall secretly into the bosom creep
Of that same noble prelate, well beloved,
The archbishop—

Hot. Of York, is't not ?

Wor. True ; who bears hard
His brother's death at Bristol, the Lord Scroop
I speak not this in estimation,
As what I think might be, but what I know
Is ruminated, plotted, and set down ;
And only stays but to behold the face
Of that occasion that shall bring it on.

Hot. I smell it ; upon my life, it will do well.

North. Before the game's a-foot, thou still let'st slip

Hot. Why, it cannot choose but be a noble plot :—
And then the power of Scotland, and of York,
To join with Mortimer, ha ?

Wor. And so they shall.

Hot. In faith, it exceedingly well aimed.

Wor. And 'tis no little reason bids us speed,

To save o r heads by raising of a head;
For, bear ourselves as even as we can,
The king will always think him in our debt;
And think, we think ourselves unsatisfied
Till he had found a time to pay us home.
And see, already, how he doth begin,
And make us strangers to his looks of love,
 Hot. He does, he does; we'll be revenged on him.
 Wor. Cousin, farewell:—no further go in this,
Than I by letters shall direct your course.
 North. Farewell, good brother; we shall thrive, I trust
 Hot. Uncle, adieu:—O, let the hours be short,
Till fields, and blows, and groans applaud our sport!
 [*Exeunt Northumberland and Hotspur*, R., *Worces
 ter*, L.

END OF ACT I

ACT II.

Scene I.—*An Inn Yard at Rochester.*

Enter a Carrier, *with a lantern in his hand*, R. U. E.

 Car. (c.) Heigh ho! A'n't be not four by the day, I'll
be hanged: Charles' wain is over the new chimney, and
yet our horse not packed.   What, ostler!
 Ost. (*Within*, L.) Anon, anon.
 1 *Car.* I pr'ythee, Tom, beat Cut's saddle, put a few
flocks in the point; the poor jade is wrung in the withers
out of all cess.

Enter another Carrier, *with a lantern in his hand*, L.

 2 *Car.* (L. c.) Peas and beans are as dank here as a
dog, and that is the next way to give poor jades the bots:
this house is turned upside down, since Robin ostler died.
 1 *Car.* Poor fellow! never joyed since the price of oats
rose: it was the death of him.
 2 *Car.* I think, this be the most villainous house in all
London road for fleas: I am stung like a tench.
 [*Catches fleas, and examines them by the light of his
 lantern.*

1 Car. Like a tench? by the mass there is ne'er a king in Christendom could be better bit than I have been since the first cock. What, ostler! come away, and be hanged, come away.

2 Car. I have a gammon of bacon, and two. razes of ginger, to be delivered as far as Charin Cross.

1 Car. 'Odsbody! the turkies in my pannier are quite starved.—What, ostler!—A plague on thee! hast thou never an eye in thy head? canst not hear? A'n't were not as good a deed as drink, to break the pate of thee, I am a very villain. Come, and be hanged:—hast no faith in thee?

Enter GADSHILL, L.

Gads. Good morrow, carriers. What's o'clock?

1 Car. I think, it be two o'clock.

Gads. I pr'ythee, lend me thy lantern, to see my gelding n the stable.

1 Car. Nay, soft, I pray ye; I know a trick worth two of that, i'faith.

Gads. I pr'ythee, lend me thine.

[*Crossing to 2d* Carrier.

2 Car. Ay, when? canst tell?—Lend me thy lantern, quotha?—marry, I'll see thee hanged first.

Gads. I say, sirrah carrier, what time do you mean to come to London?

2 Car. (R.) Time enough to go to bed with a candle, I warrant thee. Come neighbor Muggs, we'll call up the gentlemen; they'll along with company, for they have great charge.

[*Exeunt Carriers,* L., *Gadshill* R.

SCENE II.—*The Road by Gad's Hill.*

Enter PRINCE OF WALES *and* POINS, *disguised,* L.

Poins. Come, shelter, shelter; I have removed Falstaff's horse, and he frets like a gummed velvet.

P. Hen. Stand close.

[*Both retire into back scene, among the trees.*

Enter FALSTAFF, *disguised,* L.

Fal. Poins! Poins, and be hanged! Poins!

P. Hen. [*Coming forward.*] Peace, ye fat kidneyed rascal:—what a brawling dost thou keep!

Fal. What, Poins! Hal!

P. Hen. He is walked up to the top of the hill: I'll go seek him.   [*Retires again into back ground.*

Fal. (L.) I am accursed, to rob in that thief's company: the rascal hath removed my horse, and tied him ,I know not where. If I travel but four foot by the square farther a-foot, I shall break my wind. Well, I doubt not but to die a fair death, for all this; if I 'scape hanging for killing that rogue. I have forsworn his company hourly any time this two-and-twenty year, and yet I am bewitched with the rogues company. (c.) If the rascal have not given me medicines to make me love him, I'll be hanged; it could not be else; I have drunk medicines.—Poins!— Hal!—a plague upon you both! Bardolph!—Peto!— I'll starve, ere I'll rob a foot further. An 'twere not as good a deed as drink, to turn true man, and leave these rogues, I am the veriest varlet that ever chewed with a tooth. (R. c.) Eight yards of uneven ground, is three score and ten miles a-foot with me; and the stony-hearted villains know it well enough: a plague upon't, when thieves cannot be true to one another!—[*They whistle.*]—Whew! —A plague upon you all! Give me my horse, you rogues; give me my horse, and be hanged.

P. Hen. [*Back scene.*] Peace, ye fat-guts! lie down! lay thine ear close to the ground, and list if thou canst hear the tread of travellers.

Fal. Have you any levers to lift me up again, being down? 'Sblood, I'll not bear mine own flesh so far a-foot again, for all the coin in thy father's exchequer.— What a plague mean ye, to colt me thus?

P. Hen. Thou liest, thou art not colted, thou art uncolted.   [*Advances.*

Fal. I pr'ythee, good Prince Hal, help me to my horse; —good king's son.

P. Hen. (c.) Out, you rogue! shall I be your ostler?

Fal. (c.) Go, hang thyself in thy own heir-apparent garters! If I be ta'en, I'll peach for this. An I have not ballads made on you all, and sung to filthy tunes, let a cup of sack be my poison. When a jest 's so forward, and a-foot too!—I hate it.

Enter POINS, GADSHILL, BARDOLPH, *and* PETO, *disguised*, L.

Gads. (L.) Stand.

Fal. (C.) So I do, against my will.

Poins. (L. C.) O, 'tis our setter; I know his voice.

Gads. Case ye, case ye; on with your visors; there's money of the king's coming down the hill, tis going to the king's exchequer.

Fal. You lie, you rogue; 'tis going to the king's tavern.

Gads. There's enough to make us all.

Fal. To be hanged.

P. Hen. Sirs, you four shall front them in the narrow lane: Ned Poins and I will walk lower: if they 'scape from your encounter, then they light on us.

Fal. But how many be there of them?

Gads. Some eight, or ten.

Fal. Zounds! will they not rob us?

P. Hen. What, a coward, Sir John Paunch·

Fal. Indeed, I am not John of Gaunt, your grandfather; but yet no coward, Hal.

P. Hen. Well, we leave that to the proof.

Poins. (R.) Sirrah Jack, thy horse stands behind the hedge; when thou need'st him, there thou shalt find him. Farewell, and stand fast.

Fal. Now cannot I strike him, if I should be hanged.

P. Hen. Ned, where are our disguises?   [*Aside.*

Poins. Here, hard by; stand close.   [*Aside.*

[*Exeunt the Prince and Poins*, R. S. E.

Fal. Now, my masters, happy man be his dole, say I! Every man to his business.—[*They put on their masks, and draw their swords.*

Enter four TRAVELLERS, L.

Trav. Come, neighbour; the boy shall lead our horses down the hill: we'll walk a-foot awhile, and ease our legs.

Fal. &c. Stand.

Trav. Thieves! Murder! Help! [*The Travellers run across and exeunt* R., *pursued by Bardolph, Gadshill and Peto*, R.]

Fal. [*Running about with his sword drawn.*] Down

with them! cut the villains' throats! ah! whoreson cater-
pillars! bacon-fed knaves! they hate us youth: down
with them! fleece them! Young men must live: You
are grand-jurors, are ye? We'll jure you, i'faith.

                                [*Exit,* R.

Enter PRINCE OF WALES *and* POINS, *from the back ground,*
in buckram suits.

P. Hen. The thieves have bound the true men; now,
could thou and I rob the theives, and go merrily to London, it would be argument for a week, laughter for a
month, and a good jest for ever.

Poins. Stand close, I hear them coming. [*Retire again*
into the back ground.

Enter FALSTAFF, GADSHILL, BARDOLPH, *and* PETO, *with*
bags of money, R., *laughing immoderately.*

Fal. Come, my masters, let us share and then to horse
before day. [*Falstaff repeatedly holds up his booty to sur-*
vey it, and breaks out into sudden and violent fits of laugh-
ter. They sit down on the ground, in a line across C.] An
the Prince and Poins be not two arrant cowards, there's
no equity stirring: there's no more valour in that Poins,
than in a wild duck.

              HENRY *and* POINS *advance.*

P. Hen. Your money!

Poins. Villains!

     [*The Prince and Poins attack them. Gadshill, Bar-*
         dolph and Peto run away, L., *and Falstaff, after a*
         slight blow or two, runs after them, leaving the
         booty.

P. Hen. (C.) Got with much ease. Now merrily to
       horse,
The thieves are scattered, and possessed with fear
So strongly, that they dare not meet each other.
Each takes his fellow for an officer.
Away, good Ned. Falstaff sweats to death,
And lards the lean earth as he walks along:
Were 't not for laughing, I should pity him.

Poins. (C.) How the rogue roared!   [*Exeunt,* L.

SCENE III.—*Warkworth.—A Room in the Castle.*

Enter HOTSPUR, *reading a Letter,* R.

————"But, for mine own part, my lord, I could be well contented to be there, in respect of the love I bear your house."—He could be contented—why is he not, then? In respect of the love he bears our house!—he shows in this, he loves his own barn better than he loves our house. Let me see some more. "The purpose you undertake, is dangerous:" (c.)—Why, that's certain: 'tis dangerous to take a cold, to sleep, to drink; but I tell you, my lord fool, out of this nettle, danger, we pluck this flower, safety. "The purpose you undertake, is dangerous; the friends you have named, uncertain; the time itself unsorted; and your whole plot too light, for the counterpoise of so great an opposition." Say you so? say you so? I say unto you again, you are a shallow cowardly hind, and you lie. What a lack-brain is this! By the lord, our plot is as good a plot as ever was laid: our friends true and constant: an excellent plot, very good friends. What a frosty-spirited rogue is this! Why, my Lord of York commends the plot, and the general course of the action. By this hand, if I were now by this rascal, I could brain him with his lady's fan. Is there not my father, my uncle, and myself? Lord Edmund Mortimer, my Lord of York, and Owen Glendower? Is there not, besides, the Douglas? Have I not all their letters to meet me in arms by the ninth of the next month? And are they not, some of them, set forward already? What a Pagan rascal is this! an infidel!— Ha! you shall see now, in very sincerity of fear and cold heart, will he to the king, and lay open all our proceedings. O, I could divide myself, and go to buffets, for moving such a dish of skimmed milk with so honorabe an action! Hang him! let him tell the king: we are prepared: I will set forward to-night.

Enter LADY PERCY, R.

How now, Kate? I must leave you within these two hours.

Lady. (R. c.) O, my good lord, why are you thus alone! For what offences have I, this fortnight, been

A banished woman from my Harry's bed?
Tell me, sweet lord, what is't that takes from thee
Thy stomach, pleasure, and thy golden sleep?
Why dost thou bend thine eyes upon the earth;
And start so often, when thou sit'st alone?
In thy faint slumbers, I by thee have watched,
And heard thee murmur tales of iron wars:
Speak terms of manage to thy bounding steed:
Cry, *Courage—to the field!*   And thou hast talked
Of prisoners' ransom, and of soldiers slain,
And all the currents of a heady fight.
Some heavy business hath my lord in hand,
And I must know it else he loves me not.

    Hot. What, ho!—

Enter RABY, L.

Is Gilliams with the packet gone?

    Rab. (L.) He is, my lord, an hour ago.

    Hot. Hath Butler brought those horses from the Sheriff?

    Rab. One horse, my lord, he brought even now.

    Hot. What horse? a roan, a crop-ear, is it not?

    Rab. It is, my lord.

    Hot. That roan shall be my throne.—
Well, I will back him straight.—O *Espérance!*
Bid Butler lead him forth into the park.

                    [*Exit Raby,* L.

    Lady. (C.) But hear you, my lord.

    Hot. (C.) What say'st thou, my lady?

    Lady. What is it carries you away?

    Hot. Why, my horse, my love, my horse.

    Lady. Out, you mad-headed ape!
A weasel hath not such a deal of spleen,
As you are tossed with.   In faith,
I'll know your business, Harry, that I will.
I fear, my brother Mortimer doth stir
About his title; and hath sent for you,
To line his enterprise: but if you go—

    Hot. So far a-foot, I shall be weary, love.

    Lady. Come, come, you paraquito, answer me
Directly to this question that I ask.
In faith, I'll break thy little finger, Harry,

An if thou wilt not tell me all things true.

Hot. Away,
Away, you trifler.   Love ! I love thee not,
I care not for thee, Kate : this is no world
To play with mammets, and to tilt with lips ;
We must have bloody noses, and cracked crowns,
And pass them current too.   Gods me, my horse !
What say'st thou, Kate ? what would'st thou have with
     me ?

Lady. Do you not love me ? do you not, indeed ?
Well, do not, then ; for, since you love me not,
I will not love myself.   Do you not love me ?
Nay, tell me, if you speak in jest, or no.

Hot. Come, wilt thou see me ride ?
And, when I am on horseback, I will swear
I love thee infinitely.   But, hark you, Kate ;
I must not have you henceforth question me
Whither I go, nor reason whereabout :
Whither I must, I must ; and, to conclude,
This evening must I leave you, gentle Kate.
I know you wise ; but yet no further wise,
Than Harry Percy's wife : constant you are ;
But yet a woman : and, for secrecy,
No lady closer : for, I well believe,
Thou wilt not utter what thou dost not know :
And so far will I trust thee, gentle Kate.

Lady. How ! so far ?

Hot. Not an inch further.   But, hark you, Kate :
Whither I go, thither shall you go too ;
To-day will I set forth, to-morrow you.
Will this content you, Kate ?

Lady. It must, of force.   [*Exeunt, &c.*

SCENE IV.—*The Boar's Head Tavern in Eastcheap.*

Enter PRINCE OF WALES, L.

Prince H. (L. C.) Ned, pr'ythee come out of that fat
room, and lend me thy hand to laugh a little.

Enter POINS, L. S. E.

Poins. Where hast been, Hal ?

Prince H. With three or four loggerheads, amongst

three or four score hogsheads. I have sounded the very base string of humility. Sirrah, I am sworn brother to a leash of drawers, and can call them all by their Christian names, as—Tom, Dick, and Francis. They take it already upon their salvation, that, though I be but Prince of Wales, yet I am the king of courtesy; and tell me flatly, I am no proud Jack, like Falstaff; but a Corinthian, a lad of mettle, a good boy,—by the lord, so they call me,—and, when I am king of England, I shall command all the good lads in Eastcheap. To conclude, I am so good a proficient in one quarter of an hour, that I can drink with any tinker in his own language during my life. I tell thee, Ned, thou hast lost much honour, that thou wert not with me in this action. But, sweet Ned—to sweeten which name of Ned, I give thee this penny-worth of sugar, clapped even now into my hand by an under-skinner, one that never spake other English in his life, than—*Eight shillings and sixpence*, and—*You are welcome ;* with this shrill addition, *Anon, anon, Sir,*—*Score a pint of bastard in the Half-Moon,* or so. But, Ned, to drive away the time till Falstaff come, I pr'ythee, do thou stand in some by-room, while I question my puny drawer to what end he gave me the sugar; and do thou never leave calling—*Francis,* that his tale to me may be nothing but—*Anon.* Step aside, and I'll show thee a precedent.   [*Exit Poins, L. S. E.*

Poins. [*Within.*] Francis!
Prince H. Thou art perfect.
Poins. Francis!

Enter FRANCIS, L.

Fran. Anon, anon, sir.—Look down into the Pomgranate, Ralph. .
Prince H. (c.) Come hither, Francis.
Fran. My lord.   [*Stands close to the L. of Prince.*
Prince H. How long hast thou to serve, Francis ?
Fran. Forsooth, five years, and as much as to—
Poins. [*Calls at L. S. E.*] Francis!
Fran. [*Runs away.*] Anon, anon, sir.
Prince H. [*Francis returns.*] Five years! by'r lady, a long lease for the clinking of pewter. But, Francis, dar'st thou be so valiant as to play the coward with thy indenture, and show it a fair pair of heels, and run from it ?

Fran. Oh, lord sir, I'll be sworn upon all the books in England, I could find in my heart—

Poins. Francis!

Fran. [*Runs away*] Anon, anon, sir.

Prince H. [*Francis returns.*] How old art thou, Francis?

Fran. Let me see,—about Michaelmas next I shall be—

Poins. Francis!

Fran. Anon, sir. [*Runs away.*] Pray you, stay a little, my lord.

Prince H. Nay, but hark you, Francis: for the sugar thou gav'st me—'twas a pennyworth, was't not?

Fran. [*Returning.*] Oh, lord, sir, I would it had been two.

Prince H. I will give thee for it a thousand pound : ask me when thou wilt, and thou shalt have it.

Poins. Francis!

Fran. [*Standing by the Prince.*] Anon, anon.

Prince H. Anon, Francis? No, Francis; but to-morrow, Francis, or, Francis, on Thursday; or, indeed, Francis, when thou wilt. But, Francis,—

Fran. My lord?

Prince H. Wilt thou rob this leather-jerkin, crystal-button, nott-pated, agate-ring, puke-stocking, caddis-garter, smooth-tongue, Spanish-pouch—

Fran. Oh, lord, sir, who do you mean?

Prince H. Why, then, your brown bastard is your only drink : for, look you, Francis, your white canvas doublet will sully; in Barbary, sir, it cannot come to so much.

Fran. What, sir?

Poins. Francis!

Prince H. Away, you rogue : dost thou not hear them call?

[*Here they both call him—Francis stands amazed between them, and goes to neither.*

Enter HOSTESS, L.

Hos. What! stand'st thou still, and hearest such a calling? look to the guests within. [*Exit Francis, L.*] My lord, old Sir John, with half-a-dozen more, are at the door; shall I let them in?

Prince H. Let them alone awhile, and then open the door.—[*Exit Hostess, L.*] Poins!

Enter Poins, L. S. E.

Poins. [*Advancing.*] Anon, anon, sir.

Prince H. Sirrah, Falstaff and the rest of the toeives are at the door, shall we be merry ?

Poins. (c.) As merry as crickets, my lad. But hark ye ; what cunning match have you made with this jest of the drawer ? come, what's the issue ?

Prince H. (c.) I am now of all humours, that have showed themselves humours, since the old days of good-man Adam, to the pupil age of this present twelve o'clock o'clock at midnight. What's o'clock, Francis ?

Fran. [*Without,* L.] Six and eight-pence.

Prince H. That ever this fellow should have fewer words than a parrot, and yet the son of a woman ! His industry is—up-stairs, and down-stairs ; his eloquence, the parcel of a reckoning. I am not yet of Percy's mind, the Hot spur of the North, he that kills me some six or seven dozen of Scots at a breakfast, washes his hands, and says to his wife,—" Fie upon this quiet life ! I want work."—" Oh, my sweet Harry," says she, " how many hast thou killed to-day ?"—" Give my roan horse a drench," says he, and answers, " Some fourteen," an hour after, " a trifle, a trifle." I pr'ythce, call in Falstaff. (R.) Call in ribs, call in tallow.

Enter Falstaff, Gadshill, Bardolph, Peto, *and* Francis, L., *with a tankard of Sack.*

Poins. Welcome, Jack. Where hast thou been ?

Fal. A plague of all cowards, I say, and a vengeance, too ! marry, and amen !—[*Sits,* L. c.] Give me a cup of sack, boy. [*To Francis, on his* L.] Ere I lead this life long, I'll sew nether-stocks, and mend them, and foot them, too A plague of all cowards ! Give me a cup of sack, rogue. [*Poins goes to the* R.] Is there no virtue extant ? [*Drinks.*

P. Hen. [*To Poins, leaning on his shoulder,* R.] Didst thou never see Titan kiss a dish of butter ? pitiful-hearted Titan ! that melted at the sweet tale of the sun ? If thou didst, then behold that compound.

[*Pointing to Falstaff.*

Fal. You rogue, here's lime in this sack too : [*Flings it into Francis's face.*] there is nothing but roguery to be found in villainous man ; yet a coward is worse than a cup of sack with lime in it: a villainous coward.—Go thy ways, old Jack; die when thou wilt, if manhood, good manhood, be not forgot upon the face of the earth, then am I a shotten herring.   There live not three good men unhanged in England, and one of them is fat, and grows old, heaven help the while!   A bad world, I say?   A plague of all cowards, I say still.

P. Hen. [*Crossing to him.*] How now, wool sack? what mutter you?

Fal. A king's son!   If I do not beat thee out of thy kingdom with a dagger of lath, and drive all thy subjects afore thee like a flock of wild geese, I'll never wear hair on my face more.   You Prince of Wales!

P. Hen. Why, you whoreson round man! what's the matter!

Fal. Are you not a coward? answer me that: and Poins there?

[*Poins runs at him; Falstaff rises and retreats,* L.

P. Hen. (L.) Ye fat paunch, an' ye call me coward, I'll stab thee.

Fal. (L.) I call thee coward! I'll see thee damned, ere I call thee coward: but I would give a thousand pound, I could run as fast as thou canst.   [*Prince crosses to* c., *Falstaff following.*] You are straight enough in the shoulders, you care not who sees your back: call you that backing your friends?   A plague upon such backing!   Give me them that will face me; give me—a cup of sack:—I am a rogue if I drunk to-day.

P. Hen. (R. c.) O villain! thy lips are scarce wiped since thou drunkest last.

Enter FRANCIS, *with Sack.*

Fal. (c.) All's one for that.   A plague of all cowards, still say I!

[*Drinks—Francis takes the Cup, and exit* L.

P. Hen. (R. c.) What's the matter?

Fal. What's the matter?   Here be four of us here have taken a thousand pound this morning,

P. Hen. Where is it, Jack? where is it?

Fal. Where is it? taken from us it is; a hundred upon poor four of us.

P. Hen. What, a hundred, man?

Fal. I am a rogue, if I were not at half-sword with a dozen of them two hours together. I have escaped by miracle. I am eight times thrust through the doublet; four through the hose; my buckler cut through and through; my sword hacked like a hand-saw, *ecce signum.* I never dealt better since I was a man : all would not do. A plague of all cowards!—Let them speak : if they speak more or less than truth, they are villains, and the sons of darkness.

Prince H. Speak, sirs :—[*To Gadshill, &c.,* L.]—how was it?

Gads. (L.) We four set upon some dozen—

Fal. Sixteen, at least, my lord.

Gads. And bound them.

Peto. (L.) No, no, they were not bound,

Fal. You rogue, they were bound, every man of them ; or I am a Jew else, an Hebrew Jew.

Gads. As we were sharing, some some six or seven fresh men set upon us—

Fal. And unbound the rest, and then came in the other.

Prince H. What, fought ye with them all?

Fal. All? I know not ye call all; but if I fought not with fifty of them, I am a bunch of radish : if there were not two or three and fifty upon poor old Jack, then am I no two-legged creature.

Poins. [L. *of Falstaff.*] 'Pray heaven, you have not killed some of them.

Fal. Nay, that's past praying for ; I have peppered two of them : two, I am sure, I have paid : two rogues in buckram suits. I tell thee what, Hal—if I tell thee a lie, spit in my face, call me a horse—thou knowest my old ward—here I lay, and thus I bore my point : four rogues in buckram let drive at me—

Prince H. What, four? thou saidst but two, even now.

Fal. Four, Hal—I told thee four.

Poins. Ay, ay, he said four.

Fal. These four came all afront, and mainly thrust at me : I made no more ado, but took all their seven points in my target, thus.

Prince H. Seven? why, there were but four, even now.

Fal. In buckram?

Poins. Ay, four in buckram suits.

Fal. Seven, by these hilts, or I'm a villain else.

Prince H. 'Pr'ythee, let him alone : we shall have more anon.

Fal. Dost thou hear me, Hal?

Prince H. Ay, and mark thee too, Jack.

Fal. Do so ; for it is worth the listening to.   These nine in buckram that I told thee of—

Prince H. So, two more already.

Fal. Their points being broken—

Poins. Down fell their hose.

Fal. Began to give me ground : but I followed me close, came in foot and hand ; and, with a thought, seven of the eleven I paid.

Prince H. Oh, monstrous! eleven buckram men grown out of two !

Fal. (R. C.) But, as the devil would have it, three misbegotten knaves, in Kendall Green, came at my back, and let drive at me ;—for it was so dark, Hal, that thou could'st not see thy hand.

Prince H. These lies are like the father that begets them ; gross as a mountain, open, palpable. Why, thou clay-brained guts, thou knotty-pated fool, thou whoreson, obscene, greasy, tallow-keech—

Fal. What, art thou mad? art thou mad? is not the truth the truth?

Prince H. Why, how couldst thou know these men in Kendall Green, when it was so dark thou couldst not see thy hand?   Come, tell us your reason : what sayest thou to this?

Poins. (C.) Come, your reason, Jack, your reason.

Fal. What, upon compulsion?   No : were I at the strapado, or all the racks in the world, I would not tell you on compulsion.   Give you a reason on compulsion ! if reasons were as plenty as black-berries, I would give no man a reason upon compulsion, I—

Prince H. I'll be no longer guilty of this sin : this sanguine coward, this bed-presser, this horse back-breaker, this huge hill of flesh—[*Crossing* L.]

Fal. [*Following.*] Away, you starvling, you eelskin, you dried neat's tongue, you stock-fish—Oh, for breath to utter what is like thee!—you tailor's yard, you sheath, you bow-case, you vile standing tuck.—[*Still following.*]

Prince H. Well, breathe awhile, and then to it again ; and, when thou hast tired thyself in base comparisons, hear me speak but this.

Poins. (c.) Mark, Jack.

Prince H. We two saw you four set on four ; you bound them, and were masters of their wealth. Mark now, how plain a tale shall put you down. Then did we two set on you four ; and with a word outfaced you from your prize, and have it ; yea, and can show you it here in the house : —and, Falstaff, you carried your guts away as nimbly, with as quick dexterity, and roared for mercy, and still ran and roared, as ever I heard bull-calf. What a slave art thou, to hack thy sword as thou hast done, and then say, it was in fight ! What trick, what device, what starting hole canst thou now find out, to hide thee from this open and apparent shame ?

[*Falstaff hides his face with his shield.*

Poins. Come, let's hear Jack—what trick hast thou, now ?

Fal. [*Peeping over his shield.*] By the the lord, I knew ye, as well as he that made ye. Why—hear ye, my masters—was it for me to kill the heir apparent ? should I turn upon the true Prince ? [*Throws away his sword.*] Why, thou knowest, I am as valiant as Hercules : but beware instinct : the lion will not touch the true Prince. Instinct is a great matter ; I was a coward on instinct. I shall think the better of myself and thee during my life : I, for a valiant lion, and thou, for a true Prince. [*Throws down his Shield.*] But, by the lords, lads, I am glad you have the money. Hostess, clap to the door ; watch to-night, pray to-morrow. Gallants, lads, boys, hearts of gold, all the titles of good fellowship come to you ! What, shall we be merry ? shall we have a play extempore ?

Prince H. Content: and the argument shall be—thy running away.

Fal. (c.) Ah, no more of that, Hal, an' thou lovest me.

Enter HOSTESS, L

Hos. (L.) My lord, the Prince—

Prince H. (c.) How now, my lady the hostess? what sayst thou to me?

Hos. Marry, my lord, there is a nobleman of the court at door, would speak with you: he says, he comes from your father.

Prince H. Give him as much as will make him a royal man, and send him back again to my mother.

Fal. What manner of man is he?

Hos. An old man.

Fal. What doth gravity out of bed at midnight? Shall I give him his answer!

Prince H. 'Pr'ythee, do, Jack.

Fal. (L.) 'Faith, and I'll send him packing.

[*Exeunt Falstaff and Hostess,* L.

Prince H. (L. C.) Now, sirs: [*To Bardolph, &c.,*] by'r lady, you fought fair; so did you, Peto; so did you, Bardolph; you are lions, too, you ran away upon instinct; you will not touch the true Prince; no—fie!

Bard. (L.) 'Faith, I ran, when I saw others run.

Prince H. Tell me now, in earnest—how came Falstaff's sword so hacked?

Peto. (L.) Why, he hacked it with his dagger; and said he would swear truth out of England, but he would make you believe it was done in fight, and persuaded us to do the like.

Bard. Yea, and to tickle our noses with spear grass, to make them bleed; and then to beslubber our garments with it, and to swear, it was the blood of true men; I did that I did not these seven years before, I blushed to hear his monstrous devices.

Prince H. Oh, villain! thou stol'st a cup of sack eighteen years ago, and wert taken with the manner, and ever since thou hast blushed extempore; thou hads't fire and sword on thy side, and yet thou rans't away:—what instinct had'st thou for it?

Bard. My lord, do you see these meteors? do you behold these exhalations?

Prince H. I do.

Bard. What think you they portend?

Prince H. Hot livers, and cold purses.

Bard. Choler, my lord, if rightly taken.

Prince H. No, if rightly taken—halter.

Enter FALSTAFF, L.

Here comes lean Jack, here comes bare-bone.   How now,
my sweet creature of bombast?   How long is't ago, Jack,
since thou saw'st thine own knee?

Fal. (L.) Mine own knee?   When I was about thy
years, Hal, I was not an eagle's talon in the waist; I
could have crept into an alderman's thumb ring.   A plague
of sighing and grief! it blows a man up like a bladder.—
There's villainous news abroad : here was Sir John Bracy
from you father; you must to the court in the morning.
That same mad fellow of the north, Percy; and he of
Wales, that gave Amaimon the bastinado, and made Lu-
cifer cuckold, and swore the devil his true liegeman upon
the cross of a Welsh hook—What a plague call you
him?—

Poins. (R.) Oh, Glendower.

Fal. (C.) Owen, Owen; the same :—and his son-in-law,
Mortimer; and old Northumberland; and that sprightly
Scot of Scots, Douglas, that runs o' horseback up a hill
perpendicular.

Prince H. (R. C.) He that rides at high speed, and with
his pistol kills a sparrow flying.

Fal. You have hit it.

Prince H. So did he never the sparrow.

Fal. Well, that rascal hath good mettle in him; he will
not run.

Prince H. Why, what a rascal art thou, then, to praise
him so for running!

Fal. On horseback, ye cuckoo!—but, afoot, he will not
budge a foot.

Prince H. Yes, Jack, upon instinct.

Fal. I grant ye, upon instinct.   Well, he is there too,
and one Mordake, and a thousand blue caps more; Worcester is stolen away by night; thy father's beard is turned
white with the news.   You may buy land now as cheap
as stinking mackarel.

Prince H. Then, 'tis like, if there come a hot June, and
this civil buffeting hold, we shall buy maidens, as they do
hobnails, by the hundreds.

Fal. By the mass, lad, thou say'st true; it is like we
shall have good trading that way :—But, tell me, Hal art

thou not horribly afeard? thou being heir apparent, could
the world pick out three such enemies again, as that fiend
Douglas, that spirit Percy, and that devil Glendower?
Art thou not horribly afraid? doth not thy blood thrill at
it?

Prince H. Not a whit, i'faith; I lack some of thy instinct.

Fal. Well, thou wilt be horribly chid to-morrow, when
thou com'st to thy father; if thou love me, practise an answer.

Enter HOSTESS, L.

Hos. (L.) Oh, my lord, my lord!

Fal. Heigh, heigh! the devil rides upon a fiddle-stick
What's the matter?

Hos. The sheriff and all the watch are at the door
they are come to search the house: shall I let them in?

Fal. Hal, thou art essentially mad, without seeming so.

Prince H. And thou a natural coward, without instinct.

Fal. I deny your *major:* if you will deny the sheriff,
so; if not, let him enter: if I become not a cart as well
as another man, a plague on my bringing up! I hope I shall
as soon be strangled with a halter as another.

Prince H. Call in the sheriff. [*Exit Hostess,* L.] Go,
hide thee behind the arras; the rest walk up above.—
Now, my masters, for a true face and a good conscience.

Fal. (R.) Both which I have had; but their date is out,
and therefore I'll hide me.

      [*Exeunt Falstaff, Bardolph, Gadshill, and Peto,*
       R. S. E.

Enter SHERIFF, *and several* TRAVELLERS, L.

Prince H. (c.) Now, master sheriff—what's your will
with me?

Sher. (L.) First, pardon me, my lord:—A hue and cry
hath followed certain men into this house.

Prince H. What men?

Sher. One of them is well known, my gracious lord: a
gross fat man.

Trav. (L.) As fat as butter.

Prince H. Sheriff, I do engage my word to thee
That I will, by to-morrow dinner-time,

Send him to answer thee, or any man,
For any thing he shall be charged withal:
And so, let me entreat you, leave the house.

Sher. I will, my lord. Here are two gentlemen
Have in this robbery lost three hundred marks.

Prince H. It may be so. If he have robbed these
men,
He shall be answerable; and so farewell.

Sher. Good night, my noble lord.

Prince H. I think it is good morrow—is it not?

Sher. Indeed, my lord, I think it be two o'clock.

[*Exeunt Sheriff and Travellers, L.*

Prince H. This oily rascal is known as well as Paul's.—
Go, call him forth.

Poins. (R. C.) Falstaff!—Fast asleep behind the arras,
and snorting like a horse.

Prince H. Hark, how hard he fetches his breath!
Search his pockets.

[*Poins goes out R. S. E. and searches his pockets.*
What hast thou found?

Re-enter POINS, R. S. E.

Poins. Nothing but papers, my lord.

Prince H. Let's see what they be:
[*Reads.*] Item, a capon, 2s. 2d.
Item, sauce, 4d.
Item, sack, two gallons, 5s. 8d.
Item, anchovies and sack, after supper, 2s. 6d.
Item, bread, a half-penny.
Oh, monstrous! but one halfpennyworth of bread to this
intolerable deal of sack!—What there is else, keep
close; we'll read it at more advantage: there let him sleep
till day. I'll to the court in the morning: we must all to
the wars, and thy place shall be honorable. I'll procure
this fat rogue a charge of foot; and, I know his death will
be a march of twelve score. The money shall be paid
back again with advantage. Be with me betimes in the
morning; and so, good morrow, Poins.   [*Exit, L.*

Poins. Good morrow, good my lord.   [*Exit, R.*

END OF ACT II.

ACT III.

SCENE I.—*The Presence Chamber.*

KING HENRY, *seated*, C., PRINCE OF WALES *standing*, R.,
PRINCE JOHN, EARL OF WESTMORELAND, SIR WALTER
BLUNT, *with other Gentlemen, Guards, and Attendants.*

King H. Lords, give us leave; the Prince of Wales
 and I
Must have some private conference; but be near
At hand; for we shall presently have need of you,
   [*Exeunt all but the King and Prince of Wal s,* L.
I know not whether heaven will have it so,
For some displeasing service I have done,
That, in his secret doom, out of my blood
He'll breed revengement and a scourge for me :
But thou dost, in thy passages of life,
Make me believe that thou art only marked
For the hot vengeance and the rod of heaven,
To punish my mistreadings.   Tell me else,
Could such inordinate and low desires,
Such barren pleasures, rude society,
As thou art matched withal, and grafted to,
Accompany the greatness of thy blood,
And hold their level with thy princely heart ?
 Prince H. (R.) So please your majesty, I would I
  could
Quit all offences with as clear excuse,
As well as, I am doubtless, I can purge
Myself of many I am charged withal:
Yet such extenuation let me beg,
As, in reproof of many tales devised,
I may, for some things true, wherein my youth
Hath faulty wandered and irregular,
Find pardon on my true submission.
    [*Advances a little nearer the King.*
 King H. Heaven pardon thee !—Yet let me wonder,
  Harry,
At thy affections, which do hold a wing
Quite from the flight of all thy ancestors.
Thy place in council thou hast rudely lost,

Which by thy younger brother is supplied;
And art almost an alien to the hearts
Of all the court, and princes of my blood.
Had I so lavish of my presence been,
So common hackneyed in the eyes of men,
Opinion, that did help me to the crown,
Had still kept loyal to possession;
And left me, in reputeless banishment,
A fellow of no mark nor likelihood.
By being seldom seen, I could not stir,
But, like a comet, I was wondered at:
That men would tell their children, *This is he;*
Others would say—*Where? which is Bolingbroke?*
Not an eye
But is a-weary of thy common sight,
                        [Prince turns away abashed.
Save mine, which hath desired to see thee more;
Which now doth what I would not have it do,
Make blind itself with foolish tenderness. *[King weeps.*
   Prince H. (R.) I shall hereafter, my thrice-gracious
      lord,
Be more myself.
   King H. For all the world,
As thou art to this hour, was Richard then,
When I from France set foot at Ravenspurg;
And even as I was then, is Percy now.
Now, by my sceptre, and my soul to boot,
He hath more worthy interest to the state,
Than thou, the shadow of succession.
What never-dying honour hath he got
Against renowned Douglas!
Thrice hath this Hotspur, Mars in swathing-clothes,
This infant warrior in his enterprises,
Discomfited great Douglas: ta'en him once;
Enlarged him, and made a friend of him,
To fill the mouth of deep defiance up,
And shake the peace and safety of our throne.
And what say you to this? Percy, Northumberland,
The archbishop's grace of York, Douglas, Mortimer,
Capitulate against us, and are up.   *[Prince advances.*
But wherefore do I tell these news to thee?
Why, Harry, do I tell thee of my foes,

Which art my nearest and dearest enemy?

[Prince turns away.

Thou—that art like enough, through vassal fear,
Base inclination, and the start of spleen,
To fight against me under Percy's pay,
To dog his heels, and curt'sy at his frowns,
To show how much thou art degenerate.

    Prince H. [*Nearer the King.*] Do not think so; you
        shall not find it so :
And heaven forgive them that so much have swayed
Your majesty's good thoughts away from me!
I will redeem all this on Percy's head;
And, in the closing of some glorious day,
Be bold to tell you, that I am your son:
And that shall be the day, whene'er it lights,
That this same child of honour and renown,
This gallant Hotspur, this all-praiséd knight,
And your unthought-of Harry chance to meet.
For every honour sitting on his helm,
Would they were multitudes! and on my head
My shames redoubled! for the time will come,
That I shall make this northern youth exchange
His glorious deeds for my indignities.
Percy is but my factor, good my lord.
To engross up glorious deeds on my behalf:
And I will call him to so strict account,
That he shall render every glory up,
Yea, even the slightest worship of his time,
Or I will tear the reckoning from his heart.
This, in the name of heaven, I promise here :   *[Kneels.*
The which, if he be pleased, I shall perform.
I do beseech your majesty may salve
The long grown wounds of my intemperance :
If not, the end of life cancels all bands;
And I will die a hundred thousand deaths,
Ere break the smallest parcel of this vow.

    King H. A hundred thousand rebels die in this :—
       [Rises, goes to the Prince and raises him.
Thou shalt have charge and sovereign trust herein.

    Enter Sir Walter Blunt, L.

How now, good Blunt? thy looks are full of speed.

Blunt. (L.) So hath the business that I come to speak of.
Lord Mortimer of Scotland hath sent word—
That Douglas and the English rebels met,
The eleventh of this month, at Shrewsbury,
A mighty and a fearful head they are,
If promises be kept on every hand,
As ever offered foul play in a state.

    King H. (c.) The Earl of Westmoreland sets forth to-
        day;
With him my son, Lord John of Lancaster;
For this advertisement is five days old:
On Wednesday next, Harry, you shall set
Forward; on Thursday, we ourselves will march:
Our meeting is Bridgenorth: and, Harry, you
Shall march through Glostershire.
Our hands are full of business: let's away:
Advantage feeds him fat, while men delay. [*Exeunt,* L.

    Scene II.—*The Boar's Head Tavern.*

    Enter Falstaff *and* Bardolph, R.

    Fal. Bardolph, am I not fallen away vilely since this
last action? do I not bate? do I not dwindle? why, my
skin hangs about me like an old lady's loose gown; I am
withered like an old apple-John. [*Sits,* c.—*Bardolph stands
on his* R.] Well, I'll repent, and that suddenly, while I am
in some liking; I shall be out of heart shortly, and then I
shall have no strength to repent. An' I have not forgotten
what the inside of a church is, I am a pepper-corn, a
brewer's horse. Company, villainous company hath been
the spoil of me.

    Bard. (R. c.) Sir John, you are so fretful, you cannot
live long.

    Fal. Why, there is it: come, sing me a song; make
me merry. I was as virtuously given as a gentleman need
to be; virtuous enough; swore little; diced, not above
seven times a-week: went to bordello, not above once in
a quarter of an hour; paid money that I borrowed, three
or four times; lived well, and in good compass: and now
I live out of all order, out of all compass.

    Bard. Why, you are so fat, Sir John, that you must
needs be out of all compass; out of all reasonable compass, Sir John. [*Falstaff rises.*

Fal. Do thou amend my face, and I'll amend my life : thou art our admiral, thou bearest the lantern in the poop*—but 'tis in the nose of thee ; thou art the knight of the burning lamp.

Bard. Why, Sir John, my face does you no harm.

Fal. No, I'll be sworn ; I make as good use of it as many a man doth of a death's-head, or a *memento mori :* I never see thy face but I think upon hell-fire, and Dives that lived in purple ; for there he is in his robes, burning. When thou ran'st up Gad's Hill in the night to catch my horse, if I did not think thou hadst been an *ignis fatuus,* or a ball of wild-fire, there's no purchase in money. Oh, thou art a perpetual triumph, an everlasting bonfire-light ! Thou hast saved me a thousand marks in links and torches, walking with thee in the night betwixt tavern and tavern : but the sack that thou hast drunk me would have bought me lights as good cheap at the dearest chandler's in Europe. I have maintained that salamander of yours with fire any time this two-and-thirty years ; heaven reward me for it !   [*Sits again.*

Bard. 'Sblood, I would my face were in your belly !

Fal. God-a-mercy ! so should I be sure to be heart burned.

Enter HOSTESS, L.

How now, dame Partlet the hen ? have you inquired yet who picked my pocket ?

Host. [L. *of Falstaff's chair.*] Why, Sir John ! what do you think, Sir John ? Do you think I keep thieves in my house ? I have searched, I have inquired, so has my husband, man by man, boy by boy, servant by servant : the tithe of a hair was never lost in my house before.

Fal. You lie, hostess ; Bardolph was shaved, and lost many a hair : and I'll be sworn, my pocket was picked : go to, you are a woman, go.

Hos. Who, I ? I defy thee : I was never called so in mine own house before.

Fal. Go to, I know you well enough.

Hos. No, Sir John ; you do not know me, Sir John : I know you, Sir John : you owe me money, Sir John : and now you pick a quarrel, to beguile me of it : I bought you a dozen of shirts to your back.

---

* Bardolph has an extremely large red nose.

Fal. Dowlas, filthy dowlas: I have given them away to baker's wives, and they have made bolters of them.

Hos. Now, as I am a true woman, holland of eight shillings an ell. You owe money here besides, Sir John, for your diet and by-drinkings; and money lent you, four-and-twenty-pounds.

Fal. He had his part of it; let him pay.

[*Pointing to Bardolph.*

Hos. He? alas, he is poor; he hath nothing.

Fal. How, poor? [*Rising.*] look upon his face: what call you rich?—let them coin his nose, let them coin his cheeks; I'll not pay a deneir. What, will you make a younker of me? shall I not take mine ease in mine inn, but I shall have my pocket picked? I have lost a seal-ring of my grandfather's, worth forty mark.

Hos. Oh, I have heard the Prince tell him, I know not how oft, that the ring was copper.

Fal. How! the Prince is a Jack, a sneak cup; and if he were here, I would cudgel him like a dog, if he would say so.

Enter PRINCE OF WALES, L., *making signs of marching.—Falstaff meets him,* L. C.

How now, lad? is the wind in that door, i'faith?—must we all march?

Bard. Yea, two and two, Newgate fashion.

Hos. My lord, I pray you, hear me.

Prince H. What say'st thou, Mistress Quickly? How does thy husband? I love him well, he is an honest man.

Hos. (L. C.) Good my lord, hear me.

Fol. (C.) Pr'ythee, let her alone, and list to me.

Prince H. (C.) What say'st thou, Jack?

Fal. The other night, I fell asleep here behind the horas, and had my pocket picked: this house is turned bawdy house, they pick pockets.

Prince H. What didst thou lose, Jack?

Fal. Wilt thou believe me, Hal? three or four bonds of forty pound a-piece, and a seal-ring of my grandfather's.

Prince H. A trifle, some eight-penny matter.

Hos. So I told him, my lord; and I said, I heard your

grace say so : and, my lord, he speaks most vilely of you,
like a foul-mouthed man as he is: and said, he would
cudgel you.

Prince H. (L. C.) What! he did not?

Hos. (L. C.) There's neither faith, truth, nor womanhood
in me else.

Fal. There's no more faith in thee than in a stewed
prune; nor more truth in thee than in a drawn fox; and
for womanhood, maid Marion may be the deputy's wife
of the ward to thee : Go, you thing, go.

Hos. Say, what thing? what thing?

Fal. (R. C.) What thing? why, a thing to thank heaven
on.

Hos. I am no thing to thank heaven on, I would thou
shouldst know it; I am an honest man's wife: and, setting thy knighthood aside, thou art a knave to call me so.

Fal. Setting thy womanhood aside, thou art a beast to
say otherwise.

Hos. Say, what beast, thou knave thou?

Fal. What beast? why an otter.

Prince H. An otter, Sir John? why an otter?

Fal. Why? she's neither fish, nor flesh; a man knows
not where to have her.

Hos. Thou art an unjust man in saying so; thou or any
man knows where to have me, thou knave thou!

Prince H. Thou say'st true, hostess; and he slanders
thee most grossly.

Hos. So he doth you, my lord; and said, this other day
you ought him a thousand pound.

Prince H. Sirrah, do I owe you a thousand pound?

Fal. A thousand pound, Hal? a million; thy love is
worth a million; thou owest me thy love.

Hos. Nay, my lord, he called you Jack, and said, he
would cudgel you.

Fal. Did I, Bardolph?   [*Turning to Bardolph.*

Bard. (R.) Indeed, Sir John, you said so.

Fal. Yea; if he said, my ring was copper.

Prince H. I say it is copper: darest thou be as good as
thy word now?

Fal. Why, Hal, thou knowest, as thou art but man, I
dare; but, as thou art Prince, I fear thee, as I fear the
roaring of the lion's whelp.

Prince. And why not, as the lion ?

Fal. The king himself is to be feared as the lion ; dost thou think I'll fear thee as I fear thy father? nay, an' if I do, let my girdle break !

Prince. Oh, if it should, how would thy guts fall about thy knees ! Charge an honest man with picking thy pocket ! Why, thou whoreson, impudent, embossed rascal if there were anything in thy pocket, but tavern reckonings, memorandums of bawdy-houses, and one poor pennyworth of sugar candy, to make thee long winded if thy pocket were enriched with any other injuries but these, I am a villain; and yet you will stand to it, you will not pocket up wrong; art thou not ashamed ?

Fal. Dost thou hear, Hal? thou knowest, in the state of innocency, Adam fell; and what should poor Jack Falstaff do in the days of villainy? Thou seest, I have more flesh than another man; and therefore more frailty. You confess then, you picked my pocket ?

Prince. It appears so by the story.

Fal. Hostess, [*Crossing* L.] I forgive thee : go, make ready breakfast; love thy husband, look to thy servants, cherish thy guests; thou shalt find me tractable to any honest reason ; thou seest, I am pacified. Still ?—Nay, pr'ythee, be gone. [*Kisses her.—Exit Hostess,* L.] Now, Hal, to the news at court :—for the robbery, lad—how is that answered ?

Prince. The money is paid back again.

Fal. Oh, I do not like that paying back: it is a double labour.

Prince. I am good with my father, and may do anything.

Fal. Rob me the exchequer the first thing thou dost, and do it with unwashed hands, too.

Bard. [*Eagerly.*] Do my lord.

Prince. I have procured thee, Jack, a charge of foot.

Fal. I would it had been of horse. Where shall I find one that can steal well? Oh, for a fine thief, of the age of two and twenty, or thereabouts! I am heinously unprovided. Well, heaven be thanked for these rebels, they offend none but the virtuous : I laud them, I praise them

Prince. (c.) Bardolph—

Bard. (R.C.) My lord.

Prince H. Go, bear this letter to Lord John of Lancaster,
My brother John; this to my lord of Westmoreland.

[Exit Bardolph, L.

Jack,
Meet me to-morrow in the Temple-hall,
At two o'clock i'the afternoon:
There shalt thou know thy charge; and there receive
Money, and order for their furniture.   *[Going, L.*
The land is burning; Percy stands on high;
And either they or we must lower lie.   *[Exit, L..*

Fal. Rare words! brave world?—Hostess, my breakfast; come:—
Oh, I could wish this tavern were my drum!   *[Exit, L.*

END OF ACT III.

———

ACT IV.

SCENE I.—*Hotspur's Camp, near Shrewsbury.—Flourish
of Trumpets and Drums.*

Enter EARL OF WORCESTER, HOTSPUR, EARL OF DOUG-
LAS, *Gentlemen, and Soldiers with Banners &c.,* R.

Hot. (c.) Well said, my noble Scot: if speaking truth
In this fine age, were not thought flattery,
Such attribution should the Douglas have,
As not a soldier of this season's stamp
Should go so general current through the world.
By heaven, I cannot flatter; I defy
The tongues of soothers; but a braver place
In my heart's love, bath no man than yourself:
Nay, task me to the word: approve me, lord.

Doug. Thou art the king of honour:
No man so potent breathes upon the ground,
But I will beard him.

Hot. Do so, and 'tis well:—

Enter RABY, L.

What letters hast thou there?

Rab. (L.) These letters come from your father.

Hot. (L. C.) Letters from him! why comes he not himself?

Rab. He cannot come, my lord; he's grievous sick.

Hot. Sick! how has he leisure to be sick,
In such a jostling time? Who leads his power?
Under whose government come they along?

Rab. (L. C.) His letters bear his mind, not I.

Hot. (C.) His mind!

Wor. I pr'ythee, tell me, doth he keep his bed?

Rab. He did, my lord, four days ere I set forth;
And, at the time of my departure thence,
He was much feared by his physicians.

Wor. I would, the state of time had first been whole,
Ere he by sickness had been visited?
His health was never better worth than now.

Hot. (R.) Sick now! droop now! This sickness doth infect
The very life-blood of our enterprise—
'Tis catching hither, even to our camp—
He writes me here—that inward sickness—
And his friends, by deputation, could not
So soon be drawn;—
Yet doth he give us bold advertisement,
That, with our small conjunction, we should on,
To see how fortune is disposed to us: (C.)
For, as he writes, there is no quailing now;
Because the king is certainly possessed
Of all our purposes. What say you to it?

Wor. (L. C.) Your father's sickness is a maim to us.
It will be thought
By some, that know not why he is away,
That wisdom, loyalty, and mere dislike
Of our proceedings kept the earl from hence:
This absence of your fathe'r draws a curtain,
That shows the ignorant a kind of fear
Before not dreampt of.

      Hot. (L. C.) You strain too far.
I, rather, of his absence, make thus use;—
It lends a lustre, and more great opinion,
A larger dare to our great enterprise. —
Than if the earl were here; for men must think,

If we, without his help. can make a head
To push against the kingdom, with his help,
We shall o'erturn it topsy turvy down.
Yet all goes well, yet all our joints are whole
    Doug. (R.) As heart can think: there is not such a
      word
Spoke of in Scotland, as this term of fear.
                     [*Trumpet sounds,* L.

    Enter SIR RICHARD VERNON, *and two Gentlemen,* L.

    Hot. My cousin Vernon! welcome, by my soul.
    Ver. (L.) Pray heaven, my news be worth a welcome,
      lord.
The Earl of Westmoreland, seven thousand strong,
Is marching hitherwards; with him, Prince John.
    Hot. (L. C.) No harm: what more?
    Ver. And further I have learned—
The king himself in person is set forth,
Or hitherwards intended speedily,
With strong and mighty preparation.
    Hot. He shall be welcome, too,   Where is his son,
The nimble-footed, mad-cap Prince of Wales,
And his comrades, that daffed the world aside,
And bid it pass?
    Ver. All furnished, all in arms:
All plumed like estridges, that with the wind
Bated, like eagles having lately bathed:
Glittering in golden coats, like images;
As full of spirit as the month of May,
And gorgeous as the sun at midsummer;
Wanton as youthful goats, wild as young bulls.
I saw young Harry, with his beaver on,
His cuisses on his thighs, gallantly armed,
Rise from the ground like feathered Mercury,
And vaulted with such ease into his seat,
As if an angel dropt down from the clouds,
To turn and wind a fiery Pegasus,
And witch the world with noble horsemanship.
    Hot. No more, no more: worse than the sun in March
This praise doth nourish agues.   Let them come;
They come like sacrifices in their trim,
And to the fire-eyed maid of smoky war,

All hot and bleeding, will we offer them:
The mailed Mars shall on his altar sit,
Up to the ears in blood.   I am on fire,
To hear this rich reprisal is so nigh,
And yet not ours: (R.) come, let me take my horse
Who is to bear me, like a thunderbolt,
Against the bosom of the Prince of Wales: (c.)
Harry to Harry shall—hot horse to horse—
Meet, and ne'er part till one drop down a corse.
Oh, that Glendower were come !

Mer. There is more news :
I learned in Worcester, as I rode along,
He cannot draw his power these fourteen days.

Doug. That's the worst tidings that I hear of yet.

Wor. (R. C.) Ay, by my faith, that bears a frosty sound.

Hot. (C.) What may the king's whole battle reach
   unto ?

Ver. To thirty thousand.

Hot. Forty let it be :
My father and Glendower, being both away,
The powers of us may serve so great a day.
Come, let us make a muster speedily ;
Dooms-day is near ; (R.) die all, die merrily.
   [*Flourish of Trumpets and Drums.—Exeunt,* R.

SCENE II.—*The Road near Coventry.*

Enter FALSTAFF *and* BARDOLPH, L.

Fal. (c.) Bardolph, get thee before to Coventry ; fill
me a bottle of sack ; [*Gives his flask.*] our soldiers shall
march through ; we'll to Sutton Colfield to-night.

Bard. (R. C.) Will you give me money, captain ?

Fal. Lay out, lay out.

Bard. This bottle makes an angel.

Fal. An' it do, take it for thy labour ; and, if it make
twenty, take them all ; I'll answer the coinage.   Bid my
lieutenant Peto meet me at the town's end.

Bard. (R.) I will, captain : farewell.   [*Exit,* R.

Fal. [*Pointing* L. *and laughing.*] If I be not ashamed
of my soldiers, I am a souced gurnet.   I have misused the
king's press damnably.   I have got, in exchange of a hundred and fifty soldiers, three hundred and odd pounds.   I

press me none but good householders, yeomens' sons: inquire me out contracted bachelors; such as have been asked twice on the bans; such a commodity of warm slaves, as had as lief hear the devil as a drum; such as fear the report of a caliver, worse than a struck fowl, or a hurt wild duck. I press me none but such toasts and butter, with hearts in their bellies no bigger than pins' heads, and they have bought out their services, and now my whole charge consists of ancients, corporals, lieutenants, gentlemen of companies, slaves as ragged as Lazarus in the painted cloth; and such as, indeed, were never soldiers; but discarded unjust serving-men, younger sons to younger brothers, revolted tapsters, and ostlers trade-fallen; the cankers of a calm world, and a long peace; and such have I, to fill up the rooms of them that have bought out their services, that you would think, I had a hundred and fifty tattered prodigals lately come from swine-keeping from eating draff and husks. A mad fellow met me on the way, and told me, I had unloaded all the gibbets, and pressed the dead bodies. No eye hath seen such scare-crows. I'll not march through Coventry with them, that's flat. Nay, and the villians march wide betwixt the legs, as if they had gyves on; for, indeed, I had the most of them out of prison. There's but a shirt and a half in all my company; and the half shirt is two napkins tacked together, and thrown over the shoulders, like a herald's coat without sleeves, and the shirt, to say the truth, stolen from my host of Saint Alban's, or the red-nose innkeeper of Daintry. But that's all one; they'll find linen enough on every hedge.

Enter PRINCE OF WALES, *and the* EARL OF WESTMOR-
LAND, L.

P. Hen. (L.) How now, blown Jack? how now, quilt?

Fal. What, Hal? How now, mad wag? what a devil dost thou in Warwickshire? My good lord of Westmoreland, I cry your mercy; I thought your honour had already been at Shrewsbury.

West. (C.) 'Faith, Sir John, 'tis more than time that I were there, and you too: but my powers are there already. The King, I can tell you, looks for us all; we must away all night.

Fal. Tut, never fear me; I am as vigilent as a cat to steal cream.

Prince H. (L. C.) I think, to steal cream, indeec.; for thy theft hath made thee butter. But tell me, Jack— whose fellows are these that come after.

Fal. Mine, Hal, mine.

Prince H. I did never see such pitiful rascals.

Fal. Tut, tut; good enough to toss; food for powder, food for powder; they'll fill a pit, as well as better; tush, man, mortal men, mortal men.

West. Ay, but, Sir John, methinks, they are exceding poor and bear—too beggarly.

Fal. 'Faith, for their poverty—I know not where they had that: and for their bareness—I am sure, they never learned that of me.

Prince H. No, I'll be sworn; unless you call three fingers on the ribs, bare. But, sirrah, make haste; Percy is already in the field.

Fal. What, is the king encamped?

West. He is, Sir John; I fear we shall stay too long.

                       [*Exeunt Prince and Westmoreland,* R.

Fal. Well,

The latter end of a fray, and the beginning of a feast,

Fits a dull fighter, and a keen guest.   [*Exit,* R.

SCENE III.—*Another part of Hotspur's Camp.—Flourish of Trumpets and Drums*

Enter HOTSPUR, EARL OF WORCESTER, SIR RICHARD VERNON, EARL OF DOUGLAS, *Gentlemen, and Soldiers with Banners,* R.

Hot. (C.) We'll fight with him to-night.

Wor. (R. C.) It may not be.

Doug. (R. C.) You give him, then, advantage.

Ver. (R.) Not a whit.

Hot. Why, say you so? looks he not for supply?

Ver. So do we.

Hot. His is certain, ours is doubtful.

Wor. Good cousin, be advis'd; stir not to-night.

Ver. Do not, my lord.

Doug. (C.) You do not counsel well.

You speak it out of fear and cold heart.

Ver. (C.) Do me no slander, Douglas: by my life,

And I dare well maintain it with my life,

If well-respected honour bid me on,
I hold as little counsel with weak fear,
As you, my lord, or any Scot that lives:
Let it be seen to-morrow in the battle,
Which of us fears.

Doug. Yea, or to-night.

Ver. Content.

Hot. To-night, say I.

Ver. Come, come, it may not be.   I wonder much,
Being men of such great leading as you are,
That you forsee not what impediments
Drag back our expedition : Certain horse
Of my cousin Vernon's are not yet come up ;
Your uncle Worcester's horse came but to-day ;
And now their pride and mettle is asleep,
Their courage with hard labour tame and dull,
That not a horse is half the half of himself.

Hot. (R. C.) So are the horses of the enemy
In general journey-bated, and brought low ;
The better part of ours are full of rest.

Wor. (L. C.) The number of the king exceedeth ours :
For heaven's sake, cousin, stay till all come in.

                              [*Trumpets sound a parley*

Enter Sir Walter Blunt, *two Gentleman, and a flag of
        Truce,* L. *all take off their hats.*

Blunt. (L.) I come with gracious offers from the king,
If you vouchsafe me hearing and respect.

Hot. (R. C.) Welcome, Sir Walter Blunt ; And 'would
    to heaven,
You were of our determination !
Some of us love you well : and even those some
Envy your great deserving and good name ;
Because you are not of our quality,
But stand against us like an enemy.

Blunt. And heaven defend, but still I should stand so,
So long as, out of limit, and true rule,
You stand against anointed majesty !

                              [*Put on their hats.*

But, to my charge.—The king hath sent to know
The nature of your griefs ; and whereupon
You conjure from the breast of civil peace

Such bold hostilities, teaching his duteous land
Audacious cruelty : If that the king
Have any way your good deserts forgot—
Which he confesseth to be manifold,
He bids you name your griefs; and, with all speed,
You shall have your desires, with interest;
And pardon absolute for yourself, and these
Herein misled by your suggestion.

Hot. The king is kind : and, well we know, the king
Knows at what time to promise, when to pay.
My father, and my uncle, and myself
Did give him that same royalty he wears :
And—when he was not six and twenty strong,
Sick in the world's regard, wretched low,
A poor unminded outlaw sneaking home—
My father gave him welcome to the shore ;
And—when he heard him swear and vow to heaven,
He came but to be Duke of Lancaster—
My father, in kind heart and pity mov'd,
Swore him assistance, and perform'd it too.
Now, when the lords and barons of the realm
Perceiv'd Northumberland did lean to him,
The more and less came in with cap and knee ;
Met him in boroughs, cities, villages ;
Laid gifts before him, proffer'd him their oaths,
Gave him their heirs ; as pages follow'd him.
Even at the at the heels, in golden multitudes.
He presently (c.) as greatness knows itself—
Steps me a little higher than his vow
Made to my father, while his blood was poor,
Upon the naked shore at Ravenspurg ;
And now, fosooth, takes on him to reform
Some certain edicts, and some strait decrees,
That lie too heavy on the commonwealth ;
Cries out upon abuses, seems to weep
Over his country's wrongs; (l. c.) and by this face,
This seeming brow of justice, did he win
The hearts of all that he did angle for.

Blunt. I came not to hear this.

Hot. (r. c.) Then to the point :
In short time after, he deposed the king ;
Soon after that, deprived him of his life ;

And, in the neck of that, tasked the whole state ;
To make that worse, suffered his kinsman March
(Who is, if every owner were well placed,
Indeed his king,) to be encaged in Wales,
There without ransom to lie forfeited : (L. G.)
Disgraced me in my happy victories.
Sought to entrap me by inteligence ;
Rated my uncle from the council-board ;
In rage dismissed my father from the court :
Broke oath on oath, committed wrong on wrong ;
And in conclusion, drove us to seek out
This head of safety ; and withall, to pry
Into his title too, the which we find
To indirect for long continuance.   [*Crosses, c*

  Blunt. Shall 1 return this answer to the king ?
  Hot. Not so, Sir Walter : we'll withdraw a while.
Go to the king ; and let there be impawned
Some surtety for a safe return again,
And in the morning early shall my uncle
Bring him our purposes : and so farewell.
  Blunt. I would you would accept of grace and love.
  Hot. And, may be, so we shall.
  Blunt. 'Pray heaven, you do !
      [*Flourish of Trumpets and Drums.— Exeunt, Sir W.
      Blunt, Gentlemen, and his Attendants,* L. *Hotspur,
      and his friends,* R.

END OF ACT IV.

ACT V.

Scene I.—*King Henry's Tent.—Flourish of Trumpets
and ·Drums.*

King Henry, Prince of Wales, Prince John of Lancaster, Sir Walter Blunt, Sir John Falstaff,
Gentlemen, standards, and soldiers, discovered.

  King H. [*Seated.*] How bloodily the sun begins to peer
Above yon busky hill ! the day looks pale
At his distemperature.

Prince H. (R. C.) The southern wind
Doth play the trumpet to his purposes;
And, by his hollow whistling in the leaves,
Foretells a tempest and a blustering day.

            [*A Trumpet sounds a parley.*

Enter EARL OF WORCESTER, SIR RICHARD VERNON, *and*
           a flag of Truce, L.

King H. How now, my Lord of Worcester? 'tis not
    well   ——
That you and I should meet upon such terms
As now we meet: You have deceived our trust;
And made us doff our easy robes of peace,
To crust our old limbs in ungentle steel:
This is not well, my lord, this is not well.
What say you to't?
    Wor. (L.) Hear me, my liege :——
For mine own part, I could be well content
To entertain the lag-end of my life
With quiet hours; for, I do protest,
I have not sought the day of this dislike.
    King H. You have not sought it, sir! how comes it
    then?
    Fal. (R.) Rebellion lay in his way, and he found it.
    Prince H. [*To Falstaff.*] Peace, chewet, peace.
    Wor. It pleased your majesty, to turn your looks
Of favour from myself, and all our house:
And yet I must remember you, my lord,
We were the first and dearest of your friends.
For you, my staff of office did I break
In Richard's time; and posted day and night
To meet you on the way, and kiss your hand,
When yet you were in place and in account
Nothing so strong and fortunate as I.
It was myself, my brother, and his son
That brought you home, and boldly did outdare
The dangers of the time: you swore to us,
And you did swear that oath at Doncaster,
That you did nothing purpose 'gainst the state;
Nor claim no further than your new-fallen right,
The seat of Gaunt, dukedom of Lancaster:
To this we sware our aid. But, in short space,

It rained down. fortune showering on your head;
And such a flood of greatness fell on you—
What with our help, what with the absent king—
You took occasion to be quickly wooed
To gripe the general sway into your hand;
Forgot your oath to us at Doncaster;
And, being fed by us, you used us so
As that ungentle gull, the cuckoo's bird
Useth the sparrow; did opress our nest;
Grew by our feeding to so great a bulk,
That even our love durst not come near your sight,
For fear of swallowing; but, with nimble wing
We were enforced, for safety sake, to fly
Out of your sight, and raise this present head,.
Whereby we stand opposed by such means
As you yourself have forged against yourself;
By unkind usages, dangerous countenence,
And violation of all faith and troth
Sworn to us in your younger enterprise.

  King H. These things, indeed, you have articulated,
Proclaimed at market crosses, read in churches,
To face the garment of rebellion
With some fine colour that may please the eye
Of fickle changlings, and poor discontents,
Which gape, and rub the elbow, at the news
Of hurly-burly innovation;
And never yet did insurrection want
Such water colours, to impaint his cause;
Nor moody beggars, starving for a time
Of pell mell havoc and confusion.

  Prince H. In both our armies there is many a soul
Shall pay full dearly for this encounter,
If once they join in trial.   Tell your nephew,
The Prince of Wales doth join with all the world
In praise of Henry Percy: by my hopes—
This present enterprise set off his head—
I do not think, a braver gentleman,
More daring, or more bold, is now alive,
To grace this latter age with noble deeds.
For my part, (R.) I may speak it to my shame,
I have a truant been to chivalry;
And so, I hear he doth account me too:

Yet this, before my father's majesty,——
I am content that he shall take the odds
Of his great name and estimation;
And will, to save the blood on either side,
Try fortune with him in a single fight.

 King H. [*Rising.*] And Prince of Wales so dare we
  venture thee;   [*Advancing.*
Albeit considerations infinite
Do make against it:—No, good Worcester, no; (c.)
We love our people well; even those we love,
That are misled upon your cousin's part:
And, will they take the offer of our grace,
Both he, and they, and you, yea, every man
Shall be my friend again, and I'll be his:
So tell your cousin, and bring me word
What he will do:—But, if he will not yield,
Rebuke and dread correction wait on us,
And they shall do their office. So be gone;
We will not now be troubled with reply;
We offer fair; take it advisedly.
   [*Exeunt Worcester, Vernon, and flag of Truce,* L.

 Prince H. It will not be accepted, on my life:
The Douglas and the Hotspur, both together,
Are confident against the world in arms.

 King H. Hence, therefore, every leader to his charge;
For, on their answer, will we set on them;
And heaven befriend us, as our cause is just!
  [*Exeunt the King, Prince John, Sir Walter Blunt
   Gentlemen and soldiers,* L

 Fal. [*Tapping the Prince on the back as he is going,* L.]
Hal, if thou see me down in the battle, and bestride me,
so: 'tis a point of friendship.

 Prince H. (L. C.) Nothing but a colossus can do thee
that friendship. Say thy prayers, and farewell.

 Fal. (L.) I would it were bed time, Hal, and all well.

 Prince H. Why, thou owest heaven a death. [*Exit,* L.

 Fal. (c.) 'Tis not due yet; I would be loth to pay him
before his day. What need I be so forward with him that
calls not on me? Well, 'tis no matter; Honour pricks
me on. Yea; but how if honour prick me off when I come
on? How then? Can honour set-to a leg? No. Or an
arm? No. Or take away the grief of a wound? No,

Honour hath no skill in surgery then? No. What is honour? A word. What is that word honour? Air. A trim reckoning! Who hath it? He that died o' Wednesday. Doth he feel it? No. Doth he hear it? No. Is it insensible then? Yea, to the dead. But will it not live with the living? No. Why? Detraction will not suffer it; therefore I'll none of it. Honour is a mere scutcheon and so ends my catechism.   [*Exit*, L.

SCENE II.—*Hotspur's Camp.*

Enter EARL OF WORCESTER *and* SIR RICHARD VERNON, L,

Wor. O, no; my nephew must not know, Sir Richard,
The liberal kind offer of the king.
    Ver. 'Twere best he did.
    Wor. Then are we all undone:
It is not possible, it cannot be,
The king should keep his word in loving us;
He will suspect us still, and find a time
To punish this offence in other faults:
My nephew's trespass may be well forgot;
It hath the excuse of youth, and heat blood,
And an adopted name of privilege ;—
A hair-brained Hotspur, governed by a spleen:
All his offences live upon my head
And on his father's : we did train him on;
And, his corruption being ta'en from us,
We, as the spring of all, shall pay for all:
Therefore good cousin, let not Harry know,
In any case, the offer of the king.
    Ver. Deliver what you will: I'll say, 'tis so.
Here comes your cousin.

Enter HOTSPUR, EARL OF DOUGLAS, *Gentlemen, Standards, and Soldiers* R.

    Hot. (c.) My uncle is returned; deliver up
My Lord of Westmoreland.—Uncle, what news?
    Wor (R.) The king will bid you battle presently.
    Doug. (R. C.) Defy him by the Lord of Westmoreland.
    Hot. Lord Douglas, then go you and tell him so.
    Doug. Marry, and shall, and very willingly.
                        [*Exit*, R.

Wor. There is no seeming mercy in the king.

Hot. Did you beg any? Heaven forbid!

Wor. I told him gently of our grievances,
Of his oath-breaking; which he mended thus—
By now forswearing that he is foresworn·
He calls us rebels, traitors, and will scourge
With haughty arms this hateful name in us.
The Prince of Wales stepped forth before the king,
And, nephew, challenged you to single fight.

Hot. (R. C.) O, 'would the quarrel lay upon our heads;
And that no man might draw short breath to day,
But I and Harry Monmouth! Tell me, tell me,
How showed his talking? seemed it in contempt?

Ver. (L.) No, by my soul: I never in my life
Did hear a challenge urged more modestly;
Unless a brother should a brother dare
To gentle exercise and proof of arms.
He gave you all the duties of a man;
Trimmed up your praises with a princely tongue;
Spoke your deservings like a chronicle,
Making you ever better than his praise:
And, which became him like a prince indeed,
He made a blushing cital of himself;
And chid his truant youth with such a grace,
As if he mastered there a double spirit,
Of teaching, and of learning, instantly.
There did he pause: but let me tell the world,
If he out-lived the envy of this day,
England did never owe so sweet a hope,
So much misconstructed in his wantonness.

Hot. Cousin, I think thou art enamoured
Upon his follies.
But, be he as he will, yet once ere night
I will embrace him with a soldier's arm,
That he shall shrink under my courtesy.

Enter Earl of Douglas, R.

Doug. Arm, gentleman, to arms! for I have thrown
A brave defiance in King Henry's teeth
And Westmoreland, that was engaged did bear it;
Which cannot choose but bring him quickly on.

Hot. Arm, arm with speed!—

O, gentleman, the time of life is short;
To spend that shortness basely, were too long,
If life did ride upon a dial's point,
Still ending at the arrival of an hour.
And if we live, we live to tread on kings;
If die—brave death, when princes die with us!

Enter RABY, R.

Rab. I have a letter.
Hot. Away, I have not time to read them.
Rab. My lord, prepare; the king comes on apace.
Hot. I thank him, that he cuts me from my tale;
For I profess not talking: only this—
Let each man do his best: and here draw I
A sword, whose temper I intend to stain
With the best blood that I can meet withal
In the adventure of this perilous day.
Sound all the lofty instruments of war,
And by that music let us all embrace;
For, heaven to earth, some of us never shall
A second time do such courtesy.
    [*The drums, trumpets, &c. sound*—*They embrace*
Now—Esperance!—Percy!—and set on.
        [*Trumpets, drums, &c.—Exeunt,* L.

SCENE III.—*The Field of Battle near Shrewsbury.—*
        Alarums.

Enter EARL OF DOUGLAS, R. *and* SIR WALTER BLUNT, L.

Blunt. What is thy name, that in the battle thus
Thou crossest me? what honour dost thou seek
Upon my head?
Doug. Know then, my name is Douglas;
And I do haunt thee in the battle thus,
Because some tell me that thou art a king.
Blunt. They tell thee true.
Doug. The Lord of Stafford dear to-day hath bought
Thy likeness; for, instead of thee, King Harry,
This sword hath ended him: so shall it thee,
Unless thou yield thee as my prisoner.
Blunt. I was not born a yielder, thou proud Scot;
And thou shall find a king that will revenge
Lord Stafford's death.
    [*Alarums.—They fight.—Blunt is slain.*

Enter HOTSPUR, L.

Hot. O Douglas, hadst thou fought at Homedon thus,
I never had triumphed upon a Scot.

Doug. All's done, all's won; here breathless lies the
king.

Hot. Where?

Doug. Here.

Hot. This, Douglas? no, I know this face full well:
A gallant knight he was, his name was Blunt,
Semblably furnished like the king himself.
Up, and away;
Our soldiers stand full fairly for the day.

[*Alarums.—Exeunt,* R.

Enter FALSTAFF, F. L. S. E.

Fal. Though I could 'scape shot free at London, I fear
the shot here; here's no scoring, but upon the pate.
Soft! who are thou? Sir Walter Blunt:—There's honour for you! Here's no vanity!—I am as hot as molten
lead—Heaven keep lead out of me! I need no more
weight than mine own bowels.—I have led my ragamuffins
where they are peppered: there's but three of my hun
dred and fifty left alive; and they are for the town's end,
to beg during life. But who comes here?

Enter PRINCE OF WALES, *with his sword broken,* L.

Prince H. (c.) What, standest thou idle here? lend me
thy sword.
Many a nobleman lies stark and stiff
Under the hoofs of vaunting enemies,
Whose death are unrevenged: lend me thy sword.

Fal. (R.) O, Hal, I pr'ythe give me leave to breathe
awhile. Turk Gregory never did such deed in arms, as I
have done this day. I have paid Percy, I have made him
sure.

Prince H. (R. c.) He is, indeed; and living to kill thee.
I pr'ythee lend me thy sword.

Fal. Nay, Hal, if Percy be alive, thou gettest not my
sword: but, take my pistol, if thou wilt.

Prince H. Give it me; what, is it in the case?

Fal. Ay, Hal; 'tis hot, 'tis hot; there's that will sack a
city.   [*The* PRINCE *draws out a bottle of Sack.*

Prince H. What, is it time to jest and dally now?
> [*Throws it away, and exit, L.*

Fal. If Percy be alive, I'll pierce him. If he do come in my way, so; if he do not—if I come in his, willingly. let him make a carbonado of me. I like not such grinning honour as Sir Walter hath; give me life; which if I can save, so; if not, honour comes unlooked for, and there's an end.

> [*Alarums.—Exit.* L

Soldiers enter, R. U. E. and bear off Blunt's body.

SCENE IV.—*Another part of the Field of Battle.*
(*Alarums.*)

Enter PRINCE OF WALES, L. *and* HOTSPUR, R.

Hot. If I mistake not, thou art Harry Monmouth.
Prince H. Thou speakest as if I would deny my name.
Hot. My name is Harry Percy.
Prince H. Why, then I see
A very valiant rebel of the name.
I am the Prince of Wales: and think not, Percy,
To share with me in glory any more:
Two stars keep not their motion in one sphere;
Nor can one England brook a double reign,
Of Harry Percy and the Prince of Wales.
Hot. Nor shall it, Harry; for the hour is come
To end the one of us: and would to Heaven,
Thy name in arms were now as great as mine!
Prince H. I'll make it greater, ere I part from thee;
And all the budding honours on thy crest
I'll crop, to make a garland for my head.
Hot. I can no longer brook thy vanities.

> [*They fight*

Enter FALSTAFF, L.

Fal. Well said, Hal! to it, Hal!—Nay, you shall find no boy's play here, I can tell you.

Enter EARL OF DOUGLAS, L. U. E. *he strikes at Falstaff, who falls, his head covered with his shield, as if dead, near L. S. E.—Exit Douglas, R. U. E. Hotspur is wounded, and falls near R. U. E.*

Hot O Harry, thou hast robbed me of my youth;
I better brook the loss of brittle life,
Than those proud titles thou hast won of me;
They wound my thoughts, worse than thy sword my
    flesh ;—
O, I could prophesy,
But that the earthy and cold hand of death
Lies on my tongue :—No, Percy, thou art dust,
And food for——   *Dies.*
    Prince H. (*Bending over him.*) For worms, brave Percy:
fare thee well, great heart!
Ill-weaved ambition, how much art thou shrunk!
What that this body did contain a spirit,
A kingdom for it was too small a bound;
But now, two paces of the vilest earth
Is room enough :—this earth that bears thee dead,
Bears not alive so stout a gentleman.
Adieu, and take thy praise with thee to heaven!
Thy ignominy sleep with thee in the grave,
But not remembered in thy epitaph!
                  [Sees Falstaff on the ground.
What! old acquaintance! Could not all this flesh
Keep in a little life? Poor Jack, farewell!
I could have better spared a better man.
O, I should have a heavy miss of thee,
If I were much in love with vanity.
Death hath not struck so fat a deer to-day;
Though many dearer, In this bloody fray:
Embowelled will I see thee by and by;
Till then, in blood by noble Percy lie.
             [Trumpets and Drums sound twice, L.
    Fal. [*Falstaff makes several attempts to rise, but on
hearing the drums, drops under his shield again :—at
length, getting on his knees, he proceeds.*] Embowelled!
if thou embowel me to day, I'll give you leave to powder
me, and eat me too, to-morrow. [*Stands up,* c.] 'Sblood,
'twas time to counterfeit, or that hot termagant Scot had
paid me scot and lot, too. Counterfeit? I lie; I am no
counterfeit; for he is but the counterfeit of a man; who
hath not the life of a man : but to counterfeit dying, when
a man thereby liveth, is to be no counterfeit, but the true
and perfect image of life, indeed. The better part of val-

our is discretion; in the which better part I have saved
my life.—I am afraid of this gunpowder Percy, though he
be dead: how if he should counterfeit too, and rise? I
am afraid he would prove the better counterfeit; therefore, I'll make him sure; yea, and I'll swear I killed him.
Why may not he rise, as well as I? Nothing confutes me
but eyes; and nobody sees me: therefore, sirrah, [*Stabs
Hotspur.*] with a new wound in your thigh, come you along
with me. [*Falstaff here makes a variety of fruitless at-
tempts to to take up the dead body of Hotspur; at length
he sits down between the the legs of the corpse, and with one
of its arms over each of his shoulders, he is attempting to get
up.*]

Enter PRINCE OF WALES, PRINCE JOHN OF LANCASTER,
and four Soldiers, L.

Prince H. Come, brother John, full bravely hast thou
        flesh'd
Thy maiden sword.
    Prince J. But, soft! what have we here?
Did not you tell me this fat man was dead?
    Prince H. I did; I saw him dead, breathless and bleed
        ing
On the ground.—
Art thou alive? or is it phantasy
That plays upon our sight? 'Pr'ythee speak:
We will not trust our eyes, without our ears;
Thou art not what thou seem'st.
    Fal. No that's certain; I am not a double man: but if
I be not Jack Falstaff, [*Throws the body down.*] There is
Percy. If your father will do me any honour, so; if not
let him kill the next Percy himself. I look to be either
earl or duke, I can assure you.
    Prince H. Why, Percy I killed myself, and saw thee
        dead.
    Fal. Didst thou! Lord, lord, how this world is given
to lying! I grant you, I was down, and out of breath; and
so was he; but we rose both at instant, and fought a long
hour by Shrewsbury clock. If I may be believed, so; if
not, let them, that should reward valour, bear the sin upon
their own heads, I'll take it upon my death, I gave him
this wound in the thigh: if the man were alive, and would
deny it, I would make him eat a peace of my sword.

Prince J. This is the strangest tale that e're I heard.

Prince H. This is the strangest fellow, brother John.
For my part, if a lie may do thee grace,
I'll gulp it with the happiest terms I have.

                     [*Trumpet sounds a retreat.*

The trumpets sounds retreat; the day is ours.
Come, brother, let's to the highest of the field,
To see what friends are living, who are dead.

         [*Exeunt Prince Henry, Prince John,* L.

Fal. I'll follow, as they say, for reward. He that re-
wards me, heaven reward him! If I do grow great, I'll
grow less; for I'll purge, and leave sack, and live cleanly,
as a nobleman should do.

     [*Flourish of Drums and Trumpets.—Exeunt Falstaff
         and four Soldiers, bearing Hotspur's body,* I.*

SCENE V.—*King Henry's Tent.—Flourish of Drums and
                Trumpets.*

KING HENRY, *seated,* PRINCE OF WALES, PRINCE JOHN
OF LANCASTER, EARL OF WESTMORELAND, *Gentlemen
and Soldiers, with* WORCESTER, VERNON, *and others,
Prisoners.*

King H. Thus ever did rebellion find rebuke.
Ill-spirited Worcester! did we not send grace,
Pardon, and terms of love to all of you?
And wouldst thou turn offers contrary?

Wor. What I have done, my safety urged me to;
And I embraced this fortune patiently
Since not to be avoided it falls on me.

King H. Bear Worcester to the death, and Vernon
too;—Other offenders we will pause upon—

     [*Exeunt, Two Officers, Worcester, Vernon, and Four
        Gentlemen, guarded by Six Soldiers,* L. II.*

Rebellion in this land shall lose his sway,
Meeting the check of such another day;
And, since this business so far fair is done,
Let us not leave till all our own be won.   —

            [*Flourish of trumpets and drums.*

THE END.

Why is It

THAT people will neglect to provide themselves with such simple preventives as Dame Nature has placed at their disposal, until they are prostrated flat on their backs by fevers, and forced to take "peroic doses" of powerful minerals, and pay the enormous bills of doctors, when a reasonable supply of

Plantation Bitters,

taken according to directions, three times a day, will prevent each and all of the *bilious diseases* liable to attack the system during the changes which take place at the breaking up of winter and the inauguration of Spring and Summer heats.

The world is undoubtedly physiced to death. The best physicians give the least physic—and all sensible doctors will readily agree that the best way to baffle the effects, is to anticipate their insidious attacks, and with an *ounce* of preventive we save often more than a *pound* of cure. Between the retreat of cold weather and the advance of warm or cold, the whole human system undergoes a change—no greater is the metamorphosis in the physical world than it is in the human. Now, the most important mission of the medical profession is to prevent sickness, and not to cure it. Remedial agents would never be needed, provided timely antidotes were used to avert diseases.

Vegetable medicines have long been regarded as superior to mineral. The

Plantation Bitters

are composed wholly of those well-known vegetable ingredients which long ages of science and experience, (which is the best teacher after all,) have recognized as the best stomach regulators and appetizers in the known world. As a protective medicine, for male and female, old and young, these BITTERS stand alone without a rival in the known world. To enable the system to resist the ill effects of exposure to a change of climate, and as a vitalizing and strength-renewing and imparting agent, the medical fraternity have recommended PLANTATION BITTERS to their patients, as the best Tonic and Alterative, now offered to an appreciative public.

At one era in the medical world, practitioners resorted almost exclusively to powerful mineral poisons, and to blistering, bleeding, salivation, violent emetics or purgation, or to stupifying narcotics, to relieve their patients. But we are happy to chronicle the demise of all these barbarous practices. 'Tis no longer necessary to "throw the patient in fits" in order to cure him. The wonderful CALISAYA BARK, united with the other properties of the

Plantation Bitters,

if taken in time, and according to printed directions, will not only do away with the lancet, cantharides plaster, calomel, and the whole catalogue of drugs which puts money into the pockets of the apothecaries and doctors, but puts the sufferer into the hands of the undertaker—we say the BITTERS will not only do away with these evil practices and save innumerable good people from filling premature graves, but they will impart a vital energy to those who use them which, with restored health, imparts new tone and beauty to the skin ; lustre to the eye, and elasticity to the step.

Nervous Headache, Liver Complaint, &c., &c.

THE brain, being the most delicate and sensitive of all our organs, is necessarily more or less affected by all bodily ailments. A headache is often the first symptom of a serious disease. If the nervous system is affected, there is always trouble at its source in the pericranium. And it may here be remarked that as the nervous fibre pervades the entire frame, no part of physical structure can be affected without the nerves suffering sympathetically. Liver complaint of every type affects the brain. Sometimes the effect is stupor, confusion of ideas, hypochondriasis; sometimes persistent or periodical headache. In any case, the best remedy that can be taken is Plantation Bitters. In headache proceeding from indigestion or biliousness, or both, the stomachic and anti-bilious properties of the preparation will soon relieve the torture, by removing its cause. If the complaint is purely nervous—in other words, if it has originated in the nervous system, and is not the result of sympathy, the Bitters will be equally efficacious. For of all remedies, this rare combination of vegetable tonics, is the most reliable. Ladies who are subject to headache in consequence of functional derangements of a special nature, will find the Bitters a specific for the agony they endure. They require an alterative and regulating medicine to do away with the cause of pain, a tonic to invigorate the nervous system; and Plantation Bitters being at once an alterative, regulator and tonic, is exactly the preparation they need.

Plantation Bitters as an Appetizer.

WANT of appetite is a sure sign that the stomach is out of order. All persons in perfect health relish their food, and it may be regarded as a rule to which there are no exceptions, that individuals who are never hungry cannot be entirely well. To eat without enjoyment, is a penance, and sustenance taken into the stomach against the inclination, does not nourish the system as it ought to do. The best known remedy for a distaste or disinclination for food, is Plantation Bitters. A wine-glassful taken half an hour before breakfast, dinner, or supper, quickens the flow of the gastric juice, and thereby provokes hunger—for the palate sympathizes with the stomach. Nor can the appetite thus created be called a false appetite, for it is the legitimate consequence of a new energy imparted to the digestive organs by this wholesale medicated stimulant. Raw spirits are often taken to provoke an appetite, and sometimes produce that effect. But the remedy in this case is worse than the complaint, for the fiery and untempered alcohol irritates and inflames the coat of the stomach, and the reaction that subsequently takes place weakens the digestion and aggravates what was, in the beginning, merely a disinclination to eat, into a positive loathing for even the simplest aliment. It is because the Bitters permanently tone and brace the organs which assimilate the food, that the dormant appetite is quickened by their use.

Plantation Bitters

ARE the very elixir of life; mild and agreeable to the taste, and gently stimulating in their action upon all the vital organs of the human system. Sold by all Druggists of reputation, throughout the civilized world.